FROM SNOW

UNLIKELY HEROES

J. E. PACE

To Kip, my home fix-it, paramedic husband who has helped me to understand how to fix both buildings and broken bodies.

CHAPTER 1

"You guys aren't going to believe this place."

I click to send the text, wondering if it will go through when I'm this far out in the boonies.

It feels like a different world.

Hills that roll across the horizon like green waves of ocean. A small, crooked orchard with overgrown apple and peach trees, little shoots springing out everywhere.

I walk farther along the land, stuffing my phone into my pocket. This part used to be a pasture of some sort—at least that's my guess from the fencing. Horses, running along these hills—what would that be like? An old barn rises in front of me, and even though it looks like it hasn't been painted in my life-time, it still has good bones to it—standing tall against the blue sky. Even the little rooster weathervane is there, tilting from east to south with the wind.

Behind the barn is a mid-sized pond—cattails growing along the south, a bunch of brush on the other side. When I walk closer, dozens of turtles slip off the shore into the water, some diving so they can't be seen, others floating along with their heads just cresting the murky waters. A fish jumps for a bug. A heron wades in the distance. A dragonfly lands on the tall blade of grass beside me, reminding me that I'd better dust off after this, or I'll wake up with a mess of chigger welts all along my seams and bra line.

Because the beauty of the south comes with a cost. For all the pretty things you *can* see, there are hundreds of little mites and pests and molds you *can't* see.

Closer to the house, I find the garden that once was—the white picket fence gone gray long ago, an empty chicken coop at the corner, collapsed on one side, but somehow still holding the promise of fresh brown eggs.

Promise, not memory.

This was my grandmother's land.

I'd never seen it before, never set a single toe on the green, rolling hills. Never explored the old brown barn. Never run home for hot cocoa after a snow, or taken a dip in the pond with the turtles on a boiling, humid day. Never known my memaw beyond a few foggy memories of my childhood.

Because she was my father's mother. And, to be honest, I'd never really known him either. Oh, I remembered him alright. He was the type you don't forget. The smell of booze—not just on his breath, but seeping from every conceivable crevice of his body. The days he threatened to kill Mama if she didn't stop 'shoveling food into her fat face and make him something edible (ed'ble) instead'—his words, not mine.

The nights I tried to fall asleep listening to him and Mama screaming over money or women or gambling.

Again.

The mornings I woke to them screaming over breakfast and jobs and who done clogged the toilet.

Again.

Weren't hangovers at least supposed to make you sleep longer? Not Daddy. He was up bright and early with a new cuss and a new scheme.

Until one day he wasn't.

Mama found him, sprawled out on the kitchen floor—the vinyl curling up at the edges, cracking in the middle. I was maybe seven or eight years old then, and I didn't really get a good look at him. The only thing I could see around Mama's impressive mass was a brown boot, tipped to the side. The bottom was dirty, with a streak of mud that looked just like Florida. And that is what I've remembered all these years. Florida streaked along my dead daddy's boot.

I pause at a fence post and look long over the rolling horizon. To the east, I can see gray clouds, but just above me, the sky is blue like it's never known rain a day in its life.

A little like me, that blue sky, thinking if you can just look the part long enough, maybe those clouds won't ever come rolling in.

But they always do.

If you had seen me at my job, or lined me up alongside my friends Macie or Becca, you never would have guessed that I was the girl from the hills, that I was the kid with a drunk dad and diseased mama, that I was the one who understood the anatomy of chiggers and the persistence and size of a good trailer park roach.

Nope. I was the one with the sleek apartment, with the shelves of designer shoes, with the leather bags and salon hair.

Looking at it from the vantage point of Memaw's house, it wasn't too hard to see that I was the one trying to hide under a shiny exterior.

And if you work so hard to make the outside shiny, what did that say about what was underneath?

I glance down at my phone to see if one of my friends has responded. I'd wanted to come alone, so it shouldn't have surprised me to feel lonely, but it did.

Just as I'm about to tuck my phone away, Becca's name pops up, along with her text. "Your Grandma's house?"

Memaw, I correct her in my brain.

"Yeah," I text back. "Seriously, we gotta come out this weekend."

"How far, Gretchen?" Macie chimes in with her own text.

"Just over an hour."

"I'm in," Becca says.

"Me too," Macie adds.

So then, I guess the question is, Am I? Am I really in?

I never heard a word from Memaw Stevens till Mama died. That was when the letters started up, the requests for little bits of money that turned into bigger bits of money.

I didn't send it all, but here and there, if I got a little extra in my paycheck, I'd send her a twenty-dollar bill folded into a paper and tucked into an envelope. Even though I'd never met her, I had a feeling that she wasn't the type of woman with a checking account.

Now, looking at the house, that hunch is reinforced. Oh, it's an actual house, not a trailer, or even a double wide. And not even just any house. It's a gorgeous old farmhouse. Wrap around porch with moss growing up the north side, a few nails poking up that need to be hit down, but otherwise sound. A hundred-year-old homestead with every single one of those years scratched into its weathered face.

I pull my phone out again, snap a quick picture of the porch for Macie and Becca, then find the code the lawyer had given me for the lock box on the front door. Cocking my head to the side, I look at the long, skinny parlor windows, painted shut. No one could get in that way. But there are a thousand other doors to this house.

Wandering my way to the back, I find it locked, as well as two side doors, one of which looks like it used to be an old servants' quarters. I kind of laugh at the thought. Servants? For my family. How far back did we have to go that that was a thing? But just south of that servant door is a little misshapen opening—a short little door that is maybe for a type of cellar or storage room. That one wiggles when I turn the knob, opening after a bit of jiggling. I duck in through the low door and see one staircase leading up, another leading down.

When I open the lower door, I find boards barring the way, but the upper one is open and I wind my way like a thief into my own brand new house.

The stairs creak and one is starting to rot, but they hold my weight. At the top I find an attic that probably hasn't been used for generations. Old trunks and boxes scattered about. Enough spiders to cast the movie *Arachnophobia*, except that more than half of them are shriveled and dead, like everything else in this room. Dusty cracked mirror, check.

Ancient cedar chest, check. Cheap plastic Christmas tree, still in the box—a little outside the rest of the motif—but still, check.

"Horror movie, anyone?" I murmur aloud, mostly because I want to hear someone say *something*. This room gets its very own video for me to send to my friends. Just as soon as I get some reception. And then I really do get spooked and hustle myself back down the stairs and through the mini door and out to the yard.

Then back to the front, back to the perfectly respectable lock box and the somewhat respectable front door. When I get it open (it requires a shove), I'm expecting creepy furniture draped in sheets like some ghost story, and am confronted with something so much worse. Broken, sagging couches, chairs with three legs tossed to the side, a stained table, full ashtrays, empty bottles.

The only thing moderately creepy, while also being moderately touching, are the pictures of family and children hung from the walls.

In the photographs, everyone is standing together by this same old furniture when it looked just a little less old, and everyone is smiling. I wonder which of these children might be my daddy, and am troubled by the thought that I have no idea.

I guess ghosts haunt you in a variety of ways. Screaming through the halls might be preferable.

What *does* scream through the halls as I make my way toward the back of the house is a smell growing stronger and stronger. For a brief moment, I'm terrified that no one has removed the body and I'm going to stumble upon a decaying version of the Memaw I barely remember. But no. It's just a kitchen full of rotting food—all the electricity turned off. Cans are bulging in the cupboards, scraps are rotting in the sink, crawling now with larvae.

I turn away, nearly gagging, barely daring to open the refrigerator. Holding my breath, I pull on the handle. Mold growing up the sides from the devastated food. Fruit flies in agitated clusters. I shut it in a rush, and leave the kitchen, sure to shut the door as I go.

In the bedrooms, I find old clothes, yellowed sheets, even a very full cat litterbox. I scour my brain for a little cat door, hoping I won't be finding a decaying cat to go with everything else. At least the smell would blend in. But on one of the upper floors, I see it on one of those porch doors—a little flap to release the cat. And let who knows what other critters in. I don't see rats anywhere, though there are mouse droppings in the pantry.

All my romantic feelings about old houses are soaring way past the honeymoon point. And it only took a few minutes.

As I leave the house, I call the executor to talk about what might need to be done. "Are you planning to sell the house, Ms. Stephens?"

"Of course," I say.

It's the only logical thing to do. I don't live in this forsaken piece of Kentucky. I don't know what on earth I'd do with a full-size farm. I don't even know… It's then that I see the porch swing, have a seat, take off my ballet flats.

The sun is setting in the distance, over one of the hills—fire and ice mixing across the skies in streaks of gold and blue. The grasses sway by the pond and just at that moment the frogs pick up their chorus, all in unison like they do—some deep instinct drawing their voices together as if led by a master conductor. I haven't heard a sound like that for so long. The executor is saying something about real estate and selling. "But if I didn't?" I ask just as he's about to hang up the phone. "If I didn't want to sell, could I hire someone to, uh, clean the place out?"

"Sure," he says. "I could recommend some real estate agents to advise you on that sort of thing. But you'll likely have to pay cash for a clear out like that.

Probably two to three thousand dollars for a job like that."

"Of course," I say, like I have three thousand dollars sitting around to clean out moldy refrigerators. "Could you get me a solid estimate for that?"

"I'd be happy to."

I push back on the swing, let myself sway forward as the sky deepens into reds and purples. Swaying back and forth, my bare feet tucked under me. The sky sinking from color to darkness, the frog song swelling, the hoot of an owl, the glow of the fireflies all up in the trees like Christmas lights.

And then my first mosquito bite.

I slide into my shoes and hurry to my car—the fantasy of what this place might have been blinking out in the glare of my headlights.

CHAPTER 2

Saturday morning dawns through the curtains in my apartment like Saturday morning always does. No frog song. No owls. No achingly gorgeous blends of light.

And no mosquitoes, I tell myself. Or lost cell service. Or moldy fridge. Or ancient plumbing. I watch the clear stream of water flow into my glass and chug the whole thing before heating up the kettle to make myself a cup of tea.

My phone is chock full of messages from Becca and Macie. I must have lost cell coverage at some point on the drive home—an entire stream of ooohhh's and aaahhh's over the property. Can't blame them for that.

I pull off the kettle, put a mint teabag into my

mug, gaze through the gauzy kitchen curtains in the chic modern flow of my kitchen—each and every element of it curated to remind me that I wasn't a hillbilly with a drunk father and an ill mother—at least I wasn't that any longer. No. I was a manager of the nicest department store in Swallowsville. Plus I own my own side business selling lipstick and other cosmetics. Which doesn't sound too amazing until you consider that it brings me another grand a month.

Because I'm good at style. Good at color. Good at seeing what will look right on a person. Good at converting them to it. Truth be told, the conversion is the easiest part. It's getting them to trust me, to try something on that they're not used to—that's the part that's hard. But once they see what I always knew was there, well, then they're sold.

Macie calls it a gift. Becca calls it a crime. I call it a living. A living. Which is why I came to the city when Mama died. Why I created a life for myself that would let me forget the one I left behind.

At least that was the intention. But hill girls aren't good at forgetting. Maybe it's the hills that call us back. Or maybe it's just our relatives with their requests for money and grimy inheritances.

I sigh, pop a piece of bread into the toaster, scroll through my messages.

"It's amazing," Macie says.

"Now you just need a few horses," Becca says.

I pause on the thought. Horses, a stable or two. Red paint on the barn. A set of gray wicker porch chairs with soft yellow cushions.

I click off my phone. No no no no. I need a cold shower or a slap in the face, that's what I need. That land would cost tens of thousands of dollars to fix up to my standards. And then what would I do with it? Just live there alone?

Alone.

Now that both of my best friends have serious boyfriends, maybe that's what my future holds anyway.

"You've got to keep it, Gretchen." That was the last text from Becca.

I click my phone back on to respond. "A ghost house and some weedy land?"

It doesn't take long for her to text back. "Is that really what you see?"

"If anyone could do it, you could," Macie texts.

"Doesn't anyone in this text thread work?" I reply.

"Struck a chord," Becca says.

"You know it," Macie pipes in.

"Well, *I've* got to get ready for work." That cold shower is calling to me. Work. What big girls in the big(ish) city do. The whole reason I came here to begin with. To get away. To find something to do with my life. Something that didn't involve barns and horses.

"Lunch?" Macie texts.

"I won't have a break till 2:00."

"Perfect," Becca says. "I'm experimenting with intermittent fasting anyway."

ork begins with a rush of boxes. Bras for the lingerie department. Swimsuits to put on clearance. I find a blue gingham one piece that would look perfect on Becca and set it aside.

As I sort and shuffle and unbox, I greet the other employees, make my way around the store checking on things, smile and lead customers where they need to go. Even if they didn't know they needed it.

Josie is working the makeup counter this morning. She waves me over when I pass. "What color?" she asks, tipping up the chin of her first makeover appointment of the day, an older woman with pretty eyes. "I was going to do the blue-gray palette, but I'm worried about how it will look against her skin."

"You can't do too much for an old woman," the older lady says. "But I've got a hot lunch date today and want to look my best."

"New boyfriend?" Josie asks.

"Husband of forty-seven years," she replies with a twinkle in her soft blue eyes.

"Girl," I say. "We'll get you looking so fine, he'll think he just got a new girlfriend after all."

"He better not think that," she says, and we all laugh.

I tip my head to the side. She's got pretty white hair, light blue eyes, and fair skin. "I think that palette might make her look a little tired around the edges," I say. "But if you add a little pop with some gold liner…"

"I thought we weren't supposed to use shiny stuff for mature customers," Josie whispers, although she's reaching for the liner as we speak.

"Put it under the blue shadow, and add a line of dark plum on top. Then neutrals for the bulk of the lid."

Josie draws obediently and when we turn the woman around to look in the mirror, she actually gasps. "Girls," she says, though Josie and I are both women in our thirties. "I'll buy the whole shop if I can look like that every day."

"Just a liner and a few shadows," Josie says, showing her how to recreate the look herself, and winking to me as I make my way to the women's department.

Past that, I take the escalators to the second floor, and enter a dynasty of dinnerware, crystal, linens, and silver—everything a young, wealthy bride might need to make all her dreams come true.

I don't spend quite as much time here. These things cost too much for me, even with my employee discount and makeup side hustle. Though I do enjoy when new things come in—the opportunity to set up displays, or help whoever else is doing it.

"You look lost, Gretchen," Jorge says, walking past me.

"Did you get anything new?" I ask, ignoring his joke.

"Not a lot," he says. "We're barely moving the inventory among the older set and the younger couples don't want anything to do with it. It's all about Target and Amazon for them." There's a little snap of distaste in his voice.

I laugh.

"Although we did get a catalogue," he says with a twinkle in his eye.

"You know I can't resist a catalogue," I say.

"Oh, I know it."

We head to the cashier area, and I can't help but notice that he's right. There's not a single customer on this floor and he hasn't had to unlock his register yet.

"Look at these," he says, pointing toward a set of napkins.

"They're gorgeous," I reply. "I love the gold embroidery."

"Of course," he says, "but no one wants to be bothered to launder their napkins."

I mean, yes. Because, yes. No one does want to *launder* their napkins. "Can you blame them too much?" I ask Jorge.

"Maybe not for every day, but there's something special about making things extraordinary every once in a while," he says. "Linens are a dying beauty."

It's then I see the newest dinnerware in the catalogue. Almost stoneware with a country vibe and blue accents. "Look at those," I say.

"Beautiful AND practical," he replies. "They won't break easily. And look, there's a little bronze sparkle in the glaze."

"I love it," I say.

"Me too," he replies, marking the page in the catalogue with a Sharpie. "That should sell better than the china we've got right now. No one's buying it."

"I see why," I say. "It looks like it's trying to be low maintenance, without the low maintenance prices. And who wants to spend that much for something that will shatter if you drop it?"

"Should I put an order in for the stoneware?" he asks.

"Let me talk to the boss," I reply. "I'll send an email after lunch."

Lunch. I glance at my watch and hustle back to grab my purse. I'd completely lost track of time—the last five hours. Because I love what I do, I tell myself, grabbing the keys out of my bag and waving to the girl at the register.

But on my way out, I rush past the lawn furniture —the center feature a tall stone wood burner—the kind you could make pizzas in if you wanted. Or just put on the patio to cook or warm up in the cool fall days. The thing that exists to spark fantasy about warmth and flame and romance and sweaters and all the things your life might look like if you just bought this little thing. For several thousand dollars.

That kind of fantasy. Not the one that tells you you'll never once make a pizza inside this thing, not the little voice that reminds you you don't even ever eat outside, because you hate bugs and humidity. Not the type of voice that says you've never even built a fire and don't even know how you would get wood for such a thing. No. The fantasy that tells you you can and you will and you should. Buy it, that is.

I race to my car, stone fire pit in my mind.

And then it comes to me—a memory—as lonely and lost and moldy as Memaw's old farmhouse.

When I'd first started working here—I was just in the shoe department then—one of the girls I'd worked with had gotten married. I'd gone to her wedding, and it was the first time I'd gone anywhere since Mama died. And this wedding, it was out in the country. A beautiful venue in an old Victorian style house. Lights and food in the back yard for the reception afterwards. Sizzle and dazzle at every turn.

But the whole time I couldn't help thinking, "What if the napkins had been dark blue instead of periwinkle? What if the lights had been wound through the trees instead of hung? What if the grounds had been a little more sprawling for dancing, the house a little more open for visiting? What if? What if? What if?" I'd set those 'what ifs' on a shelf of impossibility.

After all, how could I own an old Victorian home like that? How could I furnish and fill it? Even if I was a whiz with color and fit and style. Even if I had a wonderful sense for space and sound. Even if I was a master at blending nature with architecture?

I whip my car into Julio's parking lot, note the new lanterns around the patio. Imagine a space like that, but bigger and grassier. With a band of frogs singing to the music of the DJ.

I try to stuff the thought back on that shelf where it had been for the last several years. Try to tell myself that it's still an impossibility. Because I still don't have a Victorian house with furnishings—just an old, disgusting farmhouse, too far out in the country for people to want to come, old and rickety and partially boarded up.

My mind tries to disrobe it, take off the boards, freshen the paint. I give my brain a little mental slap and for a second my thoughts slink away, like a stray cat, hiding in some shadow, so that after dark it can tiptoe back, tap tap tapping against my thoughts.

I'd never had a house before. Now I did. And not just any house. A farmhouse in the country with a sunset of flame and a pond full of singing frogs.

What if?

CHAPTER 3

My friends are no help whatsoever in dispelling my ridiculous fantasies.

"There's no way I could pay for it," I say.

"It's free," Becca says. "You just have to clean it up."

"I didn't send you the bad pictures," I reply. "The refrigerator had enough things growing in it that it's about to develop intelligence and walk away on its own."

"Well, that's one less thing you'd have to worry about then," Macie says.

"You guys..." I order a huge plate of pasta with giant meatballs. It's the type of comfort I'm needing with this conversation.

"But seriously," Macie says, ever the pragmatist. "What does it need?"

I shake my head, suddenly unable to put it into words. "Everything."

"Keep going," she says, spearing an olive.

"The grounds are perfect," Becca (not the pragmatist) says.

"No, they're not," I reply. "They'd need to be cut back, periodically at least, or the chiggers will go wild. They might go wild anyway. But at least in the fall, the whole twenty acres would need to be mowed."

"And?" Macie prods.

"There's a garden with no garden. A chicken coop with no chickens."

"A chicken coop," Becca squeals. "I love it more every second."

"It's literally got a rotting wall and is full of straw and probably ancient chicken poop with NO chickens," I say.

"You could get chickens easy," Becca says, accepting her salad from the waiter.

"Sure," I say. "And then someone to care for them while I'm not there. Because truly I don't care what you guys say, I'm not commuting an hour and a half every day to care for that house."

"Go back to repairs," Macie says. "One step at a time."

"There are a thousand steps," I shoot back.

"All the more reason to take them one at a time."

"The outside of the house looks fine. It needs paint and stuff, but seems sound. Probably some small repairs, spray for termites to make sure it stays sound."

Macie nods. Becca watches. I fly through the house in my mind. "Stairs up mostly good. Down to the cellar unusable and boarded up. Rooms okay. Paint, carpet, a few soft spots on the subflooring."

"You're good at this, Gretchen," Macie says.

I roll my eyes. "Bathroom, total overhaul, though I really would like to find a way to keep the old features, like the claw foot tub."

"Of course," Macie says, and I realize that for a second I started talking like that was something I would actually do, when it isn't. When it can't be.

"But the kitchen is the worst," I say quickly. "It smells like there's a dead body in there."

"Is there?" Macie—always the detective—asks.

"Not that I noticed, so...probably not."

"An inspector would let you know real quick if he finds one in the cellar," Macie says, like that's a home inspector's job. I get the impression that one of her past jobs must have involved a body found by an inspector in a cellar.

And I shudder just a smidge. Admittedly I haven't really tried to make my way into the cellar yet. "Well, I think it's just rotten food, bacteria-filled canned goods, that kind of delight. And it doesn't end there. The cupboards and shelving are rotting. They'd have to be completely torn down. The floor redone. Really nice countertops put in. If I'm honest, I'd probably have to open up a wall so that people in the kitchen could see people in the living space, and so food could be served easily. Though there is this gorgeous country dining room—big enough for a huge table."

And I'm seeing it, all of it—how it is, but also how it could be. Just like I do for our customers at the store, for the women who come to me for makeup. "But Macie," I say. "This is thousands of dollars. Tens of thousands of dollars. I'm not even sure there's enough value in the house or property to make it worth that type of investment."

"Depending on what value you put into it," Macie says. "If you just flip it, maybe not. But what if you did something else?"

I lean back, stab an enormous meatball and take a bite. "Like what?" I ask.

"Oh, I don't know," Macie says. "With that missing wall that your brain took out to entertain, I thought maybe…a little entertaining. Or a lot. You know Tad and I need *somewhere* to get married."

I stare at her, the remainder of my meatball dangling on my fork.

Married?!?

At our little table, it feels like everything has gone completely silent and then Becca squeals and then I scream and then we're hugging Macie and asking where the ring is. And she pulls it from a little box in her purse where she was hiding it. And it glitters, just like her eyes.

"You rat," I say. "To sit here and talk about the house when this was hiding in your purse."

"I had to ask Sunny and Spider for their permission first, of course." (Sunny and Spider are her cats.)

"And did they say 'yes'?" Becca asks drily.

"They were a little hesitant at first," Macie replies. "But Tad brought cans of tuna and then they caved pretty quickly. And trust me, Tad hates canned tuna with the smell and texture beating against those hyper senses of his."

"Oh, Macie," I say, looking at her hand, bejeweled now with the ring. "You've got to sketch your hand— you're so good at that."

"My own hand?" she asks.

"Of course," I say. "It'll be beautiful."

"You know," she replies. "I think I'll wait till we're married and draw both our hands—me and Tad—both our rings. Together."

I get a little teary looking at her. And I know Becca does too.

"But," she says. (Did I mention the pragmatist thing?) "Wherever shall we get married? The Courthouse? The bowling alley? My backyard? The overpriced Kiwanis ballroom? Or the Venue 52, which is nice, but is legit converted from an old Steak and Shake building. All classics here in Swallowsville. Still, I was hoping for something a little more—you know…"

"Hill country?" I say, laughing. "Cause that's what you're going to get from Memaw's house."

"With you in charge?" Macie asks, leaning forward conspiratorially. "I don't think so."

"There are hills," Becca says. "And country."

"And money, money, money that needs to exist," I say. "Where's that going to come from? And why aren't we talking about you?" I ask. "And your wedding?"

"We are," Macie says.

"When?" I ask. "Next spring?"

"We were hoping for a winter wedding, actually. Maybe February."

Becca chokes. "Are you pregnant or something? That's just six months away."

"Not pregnant," Macie says. "Just old. I've been waiting for him to propose for a year. Why wait longer to get married?"

"Then that property is definitely out," I say. "Because six months probably ups the cost."

"Kickstarter," Becca says suddenly. She's been mostly silent during the house conversation. "My sister just did one and they're amazing. You could fund the whole project."

"How?" I ask.

"Well, you just have to have enough people sign up."

"Sounds easy," I say sarcastically.

"It will be," she says. "Because for each level they pay for, they get a little something in return. From you."

"Like what?" I ask.

"Start with a lipstick," she says. "Twenty bucks. You get them wholesale, right?"

I nod.

"Then makeover consultation. $50. You won't need the makeup. Just give suggestions."

I'm listening.

"Then you keep going up. Maybe they can tour the house when it's done. That would be an upper level contribution—like $100 or something, $200 if it's a family. But you need a grand prize for a Kickstarter—something amazing. Something perfect."

"Like a party," I say. "Hosted on the grounds."

"Yes," Becca says. "Catered. Waitered. Top tier. Make it, like, $6000 or something so that it's a deal for them and you."

"That's cheaper than Venue 52," Macie says.

"Ten people who buy that is $60,000," Becca adds.

I shake my head, but I'm listening. Listening. And then I'm just shaking. My head and everything else. "It's too much. It's just too much. What am I even thinking, listening to you lunatics?"

"Well," Macie says, "you know how to eat an elephant."

"One bite at a time," Becca adds, quirking that eyebrow.

"I don't want to eat an elephant," I say.

Becca looks at my clean plate—not a speck of spaghetti or crumb of meatball left. "Oh, honey, I think you do."

CHAPTER 4

$\mathcal{A}$s I'm leaving work, my phone dings with a text. "Got a few quotes, Gretchen," the real estate agent says. "Big Sons Restoration will do it for $8000."

"The whole kitchen?" I reply, feeling just a little hopeful.

"Just the clean-up and tear out," he responds. "That way, you can strip it to the studs and sell it like that."

"$8000 seems high," I text back. "And how much would it cost for a full repair?"

"Probably 20K, with you buying the supplies."

My tongue feels dry just looking at the number on my phone. And that's just the kitchen.

"We've got another company we've never used

who will charge $6000 and about $15K for the restoration. But I can't speak to their work."

The elephant is starting to feel un-bite-able. My finger is hovering over the keys, about to tell him to have $6K guy just strip it and let's get it on the market ASAP, when he texts again. "I do have a buddy who does this stuff as a bit of a side hustle. He might be a little slower, but he's cheap."

"How cheap?" I ask.

"Well, I'm not sure he'll do that cleaning at all, but if he does, it'll be about $2000, then the cost to haul off the old stuff—another grand probably."

"And the restoration?" I ask. "If I go that direction."

"Probably another $10K. You buy supplies. And he's a little slower. This is a side job for him."

"Could he do the whole thing for $10K?" I ask, feeling insane to even be asking the question. Even if I did do a Kickstarter, I wouldn't have the money soon enough.

"Maybe if you helped with the cleaning and tear out. Or even just hauled the junk."

I stare at my phone. Daddy used to haul junk. I know my way to the dump. I know my way around rotting wood and broken furniture. I was just hoping never to have to make my way to them again.

"Let me think about it," I text. "I've got tomorrow off. Maybe I'll drive down and see what I can do myself. "

"I can send him over," he texts. "He can have a look and give you a solid number that way."

"And maybe a completion date?"

"Maybe," he texts back.

Which doesn't feel super promising.

But if I wanted to eat an elephant. And if I was going to take just that first bite. Well, this would be it.

CHAPTER 5

The drive is already starting to feel familiar. The farms I pass, the old barns, one with quilt art on the side, the two one-stop towns I slow down to go through. Speed traps, Mama always called them. She wasn't wrong.

I'd almost asked Macie or Becca if they wanted to come, but they either would have fallen totally head over heels or lost their minds when they saw the gross bits. There's something in me that wants to see it again with fresh eyes, that wants to be responsible for making the decision alone.

I take the dirt road past the house and straight to the barn. I remember seeing an old trailer in there. I figure I can probably hitch it up to my SUV and haul stuff off.

And I can.

The hitch works just fine. And when I hook everything up, the wiring is still good. One of the trailer tires is a little flat, and that's all. Fortunately, for me and that flat, I've dressed more appropriately today—in stained jeans, a ratty t-shirt, and sturdy, shapeless boots.

Within minutes, I've got the tire pumped up, the trailer hitched and ready to go. I drive slowly back to the house, ready to tackle the kitchen.

I guess that's another bite down.

By the time I get back to the back door of the house, it looks like the handyman has arrived. His truck is in the driveway, dinged and scratched along the sides—presumably from hauling jobs. When I park my SUV next to him, it looks like Marilyn Monroe standing beside Danny DeVito.

I'm expecting the man to fit that truck. Maybe an older guy in his fifties or sixties—retired and doing this for a side hustle, a little worn after a long life working manual labor—graying, calloused, hunched and leathery.

Unfortunately for me and my disheveled topknot, I'm greeted at the open door by a Greek god. Just over six foot, a slosh of dark auburn hair sweeping over his forehead, the beginnings of a beard creeping up a sharp jaw. Copper eyes gaze at me. "You must be Gretchen Stephens."

I nod stupidly.

He opens the door. Flannel shirt across broad chest, long fingers, long legs in fitted jeans—tight but not, you know, too tight.

I wander in like I've lost my ability to speak.

"Jackson," he says, by way of introduction. "One Truck Hauling."

I clear my throat, trying to find my voice. "Yes," I say, like I knew. "You're my real estate agent's friend, right? The handyman."

"Well," he says, leaving the door slightly ajar. "Let's hope so. Otherwise, you just walked into an old farmhouse with some dude who's not supposed to be here."

I want to laugh, except that I realize I have walked onto the perfect set for a chainsaw massacre. I look back at the open door.

He winks. Do killers wink?

I shake my head. "So…the kitchen? Have you had a chance to look around?"

"I got here just a few minutes ago, so not a lot of time. But, well, enough to get the gist. Kitchen re-haul, bathroom re-haul. What do you want for the other rooms?"

"Hopefully just paint and flooring," I say. "I did want to knock down the wall between the kitchen and living area. Is that something you can do?"

"Well, let's go have a look."

And then, without *too* much thought, I leave the door and follow the potential chainsaw massacre-ist into the kitchen, noticing the broad shoulders, trim waist. *Shake it off, girl,* I tell myself. He's probably got a wife and kids waiting at his own little country farmhouse. And I'm not in the market for a sordid affair with an already-spoken-for country boy. Or any kind of country boy at all.

This particular country boy is currently sniffing and scrounging around like a bloodhound. Not that it would take a bloodhound to catch the aroma of the house. It smells, if such a thing were possible, even worse than it did the other day.

"Nice place," he says, and I can't help but laugh.

"My Memaw's."

"I've seen people inherit worse. I mean, as long as the rats don't carry it away, it's got some charm."

"Are there really rats?"

"Probably not," he says. "But mice for sure."

"Ah me," I murmur, letting my accent creep in just a bit.

He looks at me and smiles.

"If I haul off a lot of this junk…" I begin.

He looks at me like he thinks I'm joking and I realize I probably don't exactly look the part, even with my work clothes on.

"Okay," he says. "If you haul off this junk…" He looks at the fridge and stove, which look like they might weigh a few gazillion pounds alone.

"Well, whatever junk I can haul off. If I clean the place up, take the cupboards off, that sort of thing… How much would it cost for you to put a new kitchen in?"

"How much work can you really commit to?" he asks. It's a carefully phrased question. Which I appreciate—not condescending, not, 'I don't believe you can do it.' Just, 'what can you commit to?'

And what *can* I commit to? With a full-time job in another city, and a little side business, and the hour-long drive.

I look around, chew on my lip. "I can clean it," I say. "I don't want to, but I can. And if I haul the fridge and stove away, I won't have to clean those. I saw a crowbar in the shed, so I can do the cabinets, I think. It's been a while, but I think I can still tear stuff apart okay. And I can haul them off too. If you could help me load things, I think I could get it to the dump. Is that possible?"

He nods, looking around. "I can get you a more specific estimate when I get home," he says. "But I know I'd want $1000 up front."

"That's all?" I ask before I realize what I'm saying.

"Yeah," he says, smiling. "Plus, it gives you time to change your mind if you decide you just want to strip this place and walk away." He winks. And I like it. I try to blink the feeling away. Wife, kids, country, I tell myself.

"I might," I say. "Just exploring options."

"Well, no matter what, we've got to tear a bunch down."

I look at the wall that connects to the living space. "Not load bearing," I murmur. "How much would it cost to tear this down too?"

"Another thousand," he says. "And you'll want something pretty if you open the room up. We can talk about it, if that's what you decide to do."

"And," I begin. "Time frame. I was hoping maybe, to have the house, um, on the market by later winter."

He scrunches up his eyes in a way that looks oddly attractive on him, the copper irises going darker when he does.

"It's impossible to say," he finally replies. "But the

kitchen. You get it torn out in a week and I'll get it put together in a month."

"An if-then agreement," I say. "I don't do my part..."

"Then I'm not bound to mine," he replies.

We smile at each other and it's kind of nice, maybe even a little electric, except for the smell of rotting food and all.

"And the refrigerator?" I ask. "Is there any chance you could help me lift it into that trailer today?"

"I've got a few other errands to run," he says. "But I'll make my way back after lunch."

"Thanks," I say, exhaling. "That would be wonderful." I move toward him to shake his hand, my boot hitting an edge of the wall. It sort of spills away and a cluster of ants scurries out.

CHAPTER 6

"Soon this place *is* going to grow legs," he says, and I can tell he's trying to breathe without smelling, just like I am.

I hope he enjoyed his lunch, because as soon as he got back, he made a huge tactical error. Before I could stop him, he opened the refrigerator.

"I wish it would grow legs," I say. "Then it could take itself to the dump."

He laughs, a full-throated joyful sound, then kind of chokes on the scent. "Dear heavens," he says, just like someone's prim grandmother would have. Not that I know a whole lot about prim grandmothers—at least not firsthand. Plenty come into the store to drop money on daughters and grandbabies.

"I'm glad we're getting it out today," I murmur.

"It's probably drawing every critter on earth to its smell. And I don't want mold or that scent to get into the wood."

"Speaking of wood," he says, heading out to his truck, presumably for a dolly. "I think under that carpet you've got some real nice hardwood."

I take a peek under the edge of the living room carpet as he bumps the dolly up the two back steps.

"Oak probably," he continues, coming to kneel beside me, shoulder to shoulder, like we're a couple of pirates, looking for gold. He runs a hand over the honey-colored wood. "Refinishing it could go a long way to restoring this place to its former glory."

"Glory, huh?" I say, and we both stand, side by side, our shoulders brushing. I step quickly back into the kitchen, into the smell, into the refrigerator situation. I look at the old fridge, wondering if it's humanly possible to move the refrigerator without touching it.

"This place was gorgeous when I was a kid," he says, coming up beside me. "We drove past it on the way to church. Goats, horses, chickens, all in the yard. Loved it."

I wouldn't know, I think, kind of resenting my whole crazy family for the fact that this stranger knows more about my memaw's house than I do.

"Ms. Maybelle really declined there those last ten years." He's walking around the fridge, like he's taking a mental measurement.

"Well, hard living will do that to you," I say.

He doesn't argue, doesn't tell me she was secretly a genteel woman who planted pansies every spring and knitted doilies. He just pushes the dolly up to the fridge.

"Thanks for helping me," I say. "Getting this thing out is going to go a long way to making this place not smell like a dung heap."

"Oh, dung heaps smell way better," he says.

I nod and we both look toward the refrigerator like we're confronting some great evil.

"Okay," he says.

I take a deep breath to gather my courage, and immediately regret the deep breath part.

We're both staring at it, stalling, not wanting to touch it, much less move it.

"It's the right choice to leave the old food in," he says. "Just know, it's gonna drip all over the trailer while you drive."

"Mercy," I mutter.

"Why don't you go on and back the trailer up."

"Okay, it might take me a sec to figure that part out. Not sure I've ever backed one up before."

"You want me to do it?"

"No, I'm gonna have to figure it out one way or another. And feel free to look around inside while I figure it out. I'll never get it with someone watching."

He laughs.

"Plus, I'd love to have an itemized quote from you," I say, pausing in the doorway. "We have to tear it out no matter what, but the rest...Well, I have to decide if I fix this place up or sell it 'as is.'"

He looks around, like he's imagining what it used to be, what it could be. I know because it's exactly the same way I'm looking at it.

On my way to the door, I tap at the wall, looking at the little hole near the floor and wondering if I've got termite damage. I open the screen door, letting out a little sigh.

"It's not so far as you think," he says. "The house I mean."

I turn, surprised he heard the sigh. He's assessing the wall between kitchen and living room, not even looking at me.

"You think?" I say.

"I do," he answers. "This place has good bones."

By the time I get back, Jackson's wiggled the fridge away from the wall and has it ready to load on the dolly. The horrible smell has transferred to his shirt and I feel a little sadness at that because he'd smelled pretty great before that. "I'm so sorry," I say.

"It's got to be done," he grunts, tipping it onto the dolly I'm holding for him.

"Your wife's going to hate me," I say, and then wonder why I said it.

"No wife," he grunts, straightening the fridge so it won't tip off the dolly. "So that part won't be a problem."

"Dog then," I say, trying to cover it up.

"Yeah, maybe that. Course knowing him, he might love it."

I'd smile if I wasn't about to gag from the smell.

Together we bump the refrigerator down the kitchen steps, then tip it onto the trailer. "You got something to secure it?" he asks, almost wiping his forehead on his sleeve and then sniffing and thinking better of it.

I'm in the same boat now too, little splatters leaking from the fridge, dripping onto my jeans, through my shirt, the scent seeping into everything.

"Too bad that shower isn't up and running," I mutter under my breath.

He glances at me sideways and for some reason I blush.

<hr>

That night, he sends over the estimate. It's actually handwritten on a small notebook that he's taken a picture of. Maybe he really is a sixty-year-old guy and I just hallucinated the other one—the fumes from the kitchen and all.

Jackson's got rows of itemization in a small, tight script. I make it bigger on my phone, and cut to the bottom line. Thousands of dollars for the basics if he does everything. Seven thousand for the kitchen. Supplies are my job to pay for no matter what. Only $5,000 if I do the tear out and clean up.

I'm not sure how long that would take, but no matter what, that's a lot of my days off spent at an old house I might sell anyway. And, truth be told, I could make a couple thousand dollars with makeup sales in a month or so anyway.

So, the logical thing would be to hire him for the very cheapest job—just $2000—tear out, then sell those good bones of a house 'as is.'

The next logical thing to do would be to hire him to do everything—it's dirt cheap after all, then charge a good price for the house with some basic renovations, and never think about the house again until I close and walk away with a pretty check in hand.

The slightly illogical thing to do would be to spend my days off ripping up cabinets and sinks, hauling junk to the dump, but still selling it and walking away with that pretty check plus $2000.

And the utterly, absolute most illogical thing in the world to do would be do the tear out myself, pay for repairs, then *keep* the house for…parties?

And as insane, illogical as that last option is, my mind—traitor that it is—wanders to pricing, to possibility.

We could do weddings, receptions, work meetings, even recitals and performances if I got a decent piano in there. Art shows, readings, trainings. Heck, goat yoga. A thousand things. A thousand price points, from a few hundred dollars to a whole lot more. It wouldn't take too much for the house to pay for itself. I mean, it would take a lot, but it is *possible.* Right?

I stop on that thought, remember that the five grand only covers the kitchen. One room. And I still have to buy supplies. That's several thousand more dollars—probably twelve to fifteen for the whole room. At *least.* Then the bathrooms, carpet tear out, paint, refurnishing. A little sheen of sweat is breaking out on my forehead.

Just getting the house ready would be more days off than I could ever swing. Wouldn't it? Not to mention that this perfect re-fab I have in my head would cost forty grand, maybe more. (Heaven only knows what the plumbing looks like.) And if I was going to use it as a reception house, well, it would have to look perfect. But to make it look perfect would be to spend more money than I can afford to lose.

My head spins in circles. Even if I could raise the funds, like Becca said, I would then have to be able to make a brand new, ambitious (and long-distance) business work.

And what about my current job? Which I love. And which I'm good at. And which pays the bills, without me worrying about termites.

I chew on all of it for a minute.

Even if a Kickstarter might work—*might*—I don't have the first idea how to start one.

And even if Jackson was willing to do the kitchen, who would I hire to do the rest? He admitted to being slow. The kitchen alone will take a solid month. But everyone else is more expensive.

And suddenly I'm chomping on a whole side rack of elephant.

I take a breath. See the farmhouse as it is. Honestly as it is.

Good bones. But just bones. It doesn't just need a pretty dress; it needs a whole reconstructive surgery. But as soon as I think it, even as I'm trying to cast the idea of keeping the house to the side, I see it—the thing it could be. That foresight that is one of my gifts. Or curses?

And then there's the issue of, well, sentiment? Do I really want to keep this house that meant nothing to me, except something I lost. Except I didn't really even lose it, because I didn't have it to lose.

Until now.

A thought that hangs there in my mind.

Something to lose.

CHAPTER 7

The next morning I call Macie. "Help," I say. "I've lost my mind. And you're the logical one. Talk me out of it."

"Gonna give me a hint about what 'it' is?" she says dryly.

"The house, of course," I say.

"And the issue is?"

"I'm thinking of keeping it."

"Why wouldn't you?"

"It's a total money pit. I just had to take this refrigerator full of rotting food to the dump. It weighed a ton. It smelled like death."

"You sure it wasn't full of body parts?" she asks.

I pause. I mean, I'm not. "I didn't really inspect what was in it closely, to be honest."

"Well, I'll try to acquit you if the case comes through."

"Okay, it probably wasn't a body," I say. "But it did smell like a dead body. Like, if Tad had been there, he might have fainted."

"Unlikely," Macie said. "He's smelled dead bodies before."

"Well, then this wasn't a body because it was worse. The worst. Anyway, I had to haul it to the dump."

"You did it alone?" Macie asks. "How big was it?"

"Well, I had a dolly," I say. "And a trailer. Plus the handyman was there to help." I try to keep my voice as even as possible.

Macie pauses for the slightest beat. "Okay, what else? Now that the refrigerator's gone. What's the hold up?"

"Cost," for starters. "And even if I did some of it myself, it would still be so much that I'd just about *have* to sell it to earn back the investment."

"Which you could," she says.

Dang it. Why'd I call the logical friend?

"And why do you have to do the work?" she continues. "It can't be worth the cost."

I have no answer.

What I definitely don't say is that I wouldn't

mind working with my hands, wouldn't mind working side by side with someone else working with his hands. Of course, I don't say it. It's ridiculous.

"I guess I thought it'd be nice to work on my memaw's house."

"The Memaw you didn't know?"

"Well, yeah."

"That's fair," she says, and I'm a little surprised.

"You think?" I ask.

"I mean, sure," Macie says. "We have connections to places. Places we know, of course, but also sometimes places we didn't, but should have."

"Wow," I say. "If detectiving doesn't work out, you should try therapy."

"We both know I shouldn't," Macie says. "But why don't we all go have a look at it this weekend? Becca and I can help a little. And get a feel for it."

"Yeah," I say. "Sure. But, you've got to believe me, Macie. It's gross."

"I believe you," she says.

But she doesn't.

a fact that becomes apparent the moment she walks into the door of the farmhouse, and then right back out. "Nope," she says. "It's gonna fall down around us. And I JUST got engaged. This isn't a house, Gretchen. It's the perfect murder. It'll look like an accident."

"I thought you were the logical one," I say.

"Excuse me," Becca says. "*I* am the one studying science."

"Yeah, yeah," I say. "But to you science is art. Anyway, I'm not trying to murder anyone, and it's got good bones."

"Who told you that?" Macie asks.

"The handyman," I say. *And me*, I don't say. But I know it, knew it before he even said it.

Macie pauses for that beat again. "Fine," she says. "But does he want to kill you?"

"Not that I know of."

"And you're sure it wasn't a body in the fridge."

"Does it smell like body?" I ask.

"No, just botulism," she says. "See, murder house extraordinaire. Dangers at every turn. All of them waiting and ready to look like a total accident."

"It *would* be amazing for Halloween events," I say, just to egg her on. And also because it would be an amazing house for Halloween events. I add haunted house to my mental list of ways to make money with this house. Hay rides. Yup. That too. Haunted hay rides. Sure, why not?

"You're not wrong," Becca says, taking a tentative look around, dusting at pictures, testing the floor with little hops. "Come on, Macie. Don't be such a scaredy cat. I haven't fallen through yet."

"Yeah, well, you weigh less than I do," Macie says.

Becca hops harder. For science and all.

* * *

I set them to work loading the ancient, ready-to-explode food onto the trailer so I can take it to the dump.

"Gretchen," Macie says. "If I've done something to offend you, something you consider worth secret murder, I'd like to apologize before one of these jars explodes in my hand—killing or permanently disfiguring me."

"If it just disfigured you, then I'd never get away with it," I say with mock menace.

"True, and Tad would never let you get away with killing me. Although it *would* be the perfect murder."

"Relax," Becca says, her arms full of jars. "Just move with care."

Right on cue, Macie drops one of the jars into the trailer, and right on cue, it explodes.

The glass pings against the sides of the trailer. We scream and duck. When we come up, peeking into the trailer, Macie says, "*Gretchen!*"

"I'm sorry," I say. "I thought you were just being dramatic."

"Are you guys okay?" Becca asks.

We look at our arms and touch our faces like we're not sure. No scratches or blood.

"Remember what I said about eating elephants?" Macie asks.

"Yes," I murmur, feeling close to tears.

"Maybe sometimes we shouldn't eat elephants."

I slump next to the trailer. "I'm really sorry."

"Don't worry about it," Macie says. "For real. But I don't know if we should keep doing those old jars. And I'm not sure you should drive with them. What if they exploded while you were moving?"

"I know," I say miserably.

Becca is gazing at the jars. "Let's take them— carefully, one by one, out of the trailer, so she can at least use it again."

"No," I say. "We can't have Macie disfigured for

her wedding." A wedding that will not happen in this beautiful house.

"What are you going to do with them?" Becca asks. "They can't stay here forever."

And what am I going to do? Ask someone else to do it, make them take the risk? Are there people who specialize in disposing of ancient, explosive food? It seems unlikely. I gaze through the back door, then get an idea. "The carpet," I say.

"Carpet?" Macie asks.

If we pull it out, then wrap the jars inside, we won't have to worry about them exploding. Plus, it's got to come out anyway.

Becca and Macie look at each other. "Sure," Becca says. "But how do we remove carpet?"

"Oh," I say. "Well, you've just got to disconnect it from the tack strips from the floor by the wall. Then it'll roll up just fine and we'll drag it out here.

"How do you even know this?" Becca asks.

"I know a lot of weird things," I reply, leading them back inside and away from any murderous jars. "Here, let's each of us take a hammer." I dig through my old tool box. "We'll use the nail removing side to get the edges of the carpet up."

I drag my friends into the living room, shoving furniture out of the way and carrying light things into the bedrooms before kneeling on the floor by a wall. "Like this." I pop a bit of carpet off of the tack strip.

"But why remove the carpet if you're just going to sell it as is," Macie asks, kneeling next to another wall and settling the nail removing side under an edge of carpet.

I don't reply, intent on my carpet ripping. "Hmmm?" I finally ask as though I didn't hear.

Becca pops a bit of carpet off, moving down the wall. "Kind of satisfying, actually."

"Weirdly so," Macie adds, getting her first bit up.

It *is* satisfying. In more than one way. Because underneath the horrible avocado shag carpet is slightly dull, slightly distressed, one hundred percent original wood floor. Just like Jackson said.

"Well, that's not the worst," Becca says, looking at it with me.

"Doesn't even smell like cat pee," Macie adds helpfully, and we laugh.

"You girls ready to roll this thing up so we can move it out back?" I ask.

"Why not?" they say.

We make a sloppy carpet burrito, shoving and scooting it out of the house. We then unroll it and remove the jars (like fragile jar babies) and set them gently one by one onto the carpet, rolling as we go.

When we're done, I realize that we should have put the carpet on the trailer *before* putting the jars in and rolling it up.

I sit in the dirt on the ground, creating a little puff of dust. "Maybe you're right, Macie. Some elephants aren't worth eating."

She sits beside me, then Becca does too. Three sweaty women doing work for free.

"Should we just wait here until it all explodes?" I ask. I know that to fix it we'll have to unroll it, take the jars off again, then move it onto the trailer and load it again. And I can already feel the tears heating up in my eyes.

"You don't have to keep the house," Macie says when the first tear drops. "I know it's sentimental to you and all, but it's not a duty you have to your memaw. She's in a place where she surely doesn't care."

I nod, unable to answer, unable to explain that it's not really my memaw I was hoping to connect with, not exactly, but some part of my past that all of this represents. And how would fixing up a house really connect any of that anyway?

Becca reaches up to wipe the next tear.

"It's not exactly sentimental," I mutter.

"Then what is it?" Becca asks.

I don't answer. Instead I say, "Why don't you guys go into town and grab a pizza for us to eat?"

"And leave you to face the murder house on your own?" Macie asks.

"Yes, please," I say. Now more tears are falling.

"You sure?" Becca murmurs.

I nod.

They go, each of them casting backwards glances.

When they're gone, I sit in the dirt crying for a few more minutes. And then, still in the same spot, I unroll one edge of the carpet, remove the one jar that is cradled there, unroll a bit more. The tears are blurring my vision just a bit, and I still don't stand up, but I do scooch a little closer to the carpet, unrolling a little more, taking out a few more jars.

One jar. One piece. One bite at a time. It's true that there are some elephants you shouldn't eat. But it's also true that when I've removed all the jars, dragged the carpet onto the trailer, and then re-rolled the jars into its little jelly roll of an inside, I feel a sense of accomplishment. About throwing away old food.

Maybe that's weird, but it gives me time to go inside, walk through the carpet-less room, bend down and smell the wood. I can smell it—not moldy house, not cat pee, not dead-body-refrigerator, just old, old wood and dust. I take a bit of sandpaper out of my pocket, scrape away at the floor, and see it— the beautiful golden oak.

By the time my friends return nearly fifty minutes later with a pepperoni pizza and a bouquet of grocery store flowers, I've cleaned out the rest of the kitchen, wiping the counters, sweeping the floor. Now, instead of death or botulism, the place smells like bleach.

"Girl," Becca says, when she steps in.

"I'm starving, let's—" Macie freezes mid-sentence, looking around at the old kitchen. "Well I'll be…"

"One bite at a time," I say to her.

"You know you don't have to eat it," she reminds me.

"I know," I say. "But I'm a little like you."

"Uh, how so?" Macie asks. "I've been complaining the whole time. Also, I stole the first piece of pizza on the drive back."

I giggle, then reply, "Because I also cannot resist a tough case."

"This is a very tough case," Macie warns, helping herself to a second piece of pizza.

"You might recall," I remind her, "that once upon a time, this grumpy woman came to my store looking for a dress for her very first gala."

"Grumpy?" Macie says. "Me? I was so cooperative."

"You were an irresistible project, with your lack of knowledge about what color would look good on your skin, what shape would look good on your body, what fabric would be comfortable enough to make it through the night."

"Uh, I got stuck on the whole dress-buying part," Macie says. "I couldn't even think about color."

"Exactly," I say.

"But this house," Macie says, gesturing with her slice of pizza. "It's worse than me. Please tell me fixing this house will be worse than finding a dress for me."

"A little," I concede.

Macie gives me a we-are-not-amused look and takes a bite of pizza.

"But look at it, really look," I say. "The lines are there—the curves and edges. Look at the scalloping, the shape of the doors, the inlaid bookshelves. Classic features. Timeless beauty. Just like you." I wink. "I just have to help this house uncover it."

"You *are* good at that," Macie admits grudgingly.

"Kind of great," Becca says.

"I can see," I say. "See what this house *could* be. And seeing that, I can't now abandon it. At least without giving it a shot."

"Okay," Macie says. "One bite."

"Right," I say, turning to Becca. "Now tell me more about Kickstarters."

CHAPTER 8

"First off," Becca is saying. "If you fix it, video it."

"Uh, why?"

"You can use the videos for teasers for the Kickstarter. Before and after type things. But also put them up on YouTube. It's great advertising for the upcoming house and you might make a little side money. I mean, YouTube isn't easy to succeed on, but frankly, if you can transform this place—and if anyone can, it's you—well, I'd watch. Even though YouTube will never know the evil of its former smell."

Outside the sun is beginning to set, stretching its rays like arms across the hills. Macie is staring at it.

"Here, hand me your phone," Becca says, clicking over to the camera and taking a video.

"There, first one," she says, handing my phone back to me. "You could try TikTok too. It's all the rage."

"Isn't it just for teens?" I ask. "And dancing."

"Nah, everyone's on there now," Becca says. "It's a good idea."

"#murderhouseproject," Macie snickers.

"Yeah, that'll draw the right crowd," I reply.

"Is the electric hooked up?" Becca asks. "Because it is getting seriously creepy in here with the light fading."

"I don't even know," I say. "But I'm sure there are some melty candles somewhere to go with the murder house motif."

"No doubt," Macie says as the sun drops behind the hill, the wind picks up, and we hear a knock at the door.

Everyone jumps.

"Hello," a male voice calls. A voice I think I recognize with that sweet drawl. "Anybody home?"

I stand up.

"Are you seriously going to answer that?" Becca whispers.

"I think it's the handyman."

"Does he have a chainsaw?" Becca hisses.

"Shhhh."

I peek through a small crack in the front door. Jackson is standing there, hands in his pockets, the wind picking up around him, blowing the auburn hair across his face. I throw open the door. "Hi, Jackson."

"Oh, it's you," he says.

"Who else would it be?"

"One of the neighbors called me saying they'd heard a shot a while ago. They were worried someone was over here. Maybe a squatter or something."

"A gunshot?" I say, then remember the pop of the jar, then laugh.

"Were you shooting?" he asks.

"Nah," I say, letting my own Kentucky drip in. "My friends and I were moving old jars to the trailer and one exploded. It did sound a lot like a shot."

"Looks like I missed the fun," he says.

"You have no idea."

And then he stays there on the stoop for a second, and before I can think about what I'm doing, I open the door wider. "Do you want to come in? We had a pizza. I think there might be a slice or two left."

"I'll leave the pizza for you and your friends," he says, stepping into the living room and stopping at the carpetless-ness. "Well, I'll be."

"Different, huh?"

"I knew this place had good bones."

"Oak," I say.

"Or walnut," he adds, stooping down, just like I did. "That woulda cost a pretty penny."

I look through the doorway into the kitchen. It really is getting dark fast. "Looks like the electric isn't turned on," I say. "Guess I should have thought about that."

"There's a lot to think about with a house like this."

"You can say that again," Macie says, coming out of the kitchen and extending her hand. "Good to meet you."

"Macie, Jackson," I say, by way of introduction. "And Becca's still back in the kitchen."

"We've got a bit of a drive," Macie says, like she's my mother shooing an unwanted boy away.

"No worries, ladies," Jackson says as Becca peeks out. "Just wanted to make sure everything was good. You can call Southern Electric about the power, though I'll send you the name of a good electrician first. In case they turned it off on account of things not being safe and all."

"Murder house strikes again," I hear Macie mutter under her breath.

Jackson walks back to the door, holding it open for all of us. I stop at the lock box and put the key back.

"Looks like you got the kitchen ready for tear out," he says.

"You know," I say, looking into the coppers of his eyes. "I think I did."

"*That* is your handyman," Becca squeals as we all pile into my car.

"Yeah," I say. "What about it?"

"What about it?" Macie mimics, pitching her voice up a little higher.

"He looks like he belongs in a movie. And his voice is like velvet. I could listen to it all day."

"Better not tell Lance," I reply.

"I'm telling him as soon as I can. I can't believe you hid this guy from us."

"Hid him?" I say. "We've only met once."

"And NO mention. Come on," Becca says. "That's suspicious."

"He's cute," I admit.

"And…" Macie says, hearing the pause.

"Completely country," I say. "Just because I'm fixing this house up doesn't mean I want some guy who just does odd jobs and is living in his granddaddy's old trailer. No matter how hot he is. Or how nice."

"Nothing wrong with going country," Becca says.

"And you won't need his granddaddy's trailer," Macie adds. "You'll have murder house."

"I worked hard to get out of the country," I say.

"You make it sound like we live in New York City," Becca laughs.

"Compared to this town," I say, "Swallowsville *is* New York City."

"I don't know," Macie says, the twitch of a smile at her lips. "This little town's got good bones."

"It's not the only thing that's got good bones," Becca murmurs, snickering.

"Who cares about bones?" I ask.

"Bones are what hold all those muscles up," Becca says.

"And that hair," Macie adds. "Those hands."

"We don't all have a thing for hands," I say.

"Well, we all should," she replies. "But sure, just hire him as your *handyman*." Then she stops, snorts out a laugh. "Oh my gosh. Get it. Hand-y man. I'm brilliant."

"Yeah," I say. "Brilliant. Exactly the word I was going to use. But I think I'll just keep him as my repair man."

"Sure, sure," Becca says. "You do that."

"I'm not going country," I say stubbornly.

They both cast teasing glances at me, but I mean it. I'm not going country. I grew up with boys like that.

I'm not talking the kids who had plans for college or to take over their Daddy's business or the ones headed to the military. I'm talking about the other ones. The friendly football player ones who drank on the weekends and told glory stories that are probably still the only stories they know how to tell. The ones whose only plans were to find a hot cheerleader, get her pregnant (before or after they got married—they weren't particular), settle into a trailer, and work odd jobs for the rest of forever. The type of guy my dad started off as before everything went off the rails.

And I don't care what kind of bones you have—muscle-holding or otherwise—that kind of country guy is not the one I want. Not even close.

CHAPTER 9

Monday morning, I'm back at work. Checking inventory, checking employees, checking email.

It's on that part that I stop.

Because in the email from my boss, right under the first few sentences with permission to get the stoneware, is another paragraph. A fat, chunky paragraph.

There's an opportunity, it says, an opportunity working in corporate.

I lean in, squint at the letters like they might change if I do. They don't.

"I'd take it myself," my boss Joannah has written. "But as you know I'm about to pop out these twins and I'm trying to take a step back, not forward. But you…"

I lean back in my seat, staring at the computer.

"You'd be perfect. I'm not even sure you'd have to move to Louisville for it because most of it would involve traveling around to different stores. Of course, if you got the job, you could move to Louisville with that fat new income, and get a really nice place. Anyway, I'm getting ahead of myself, but I can't imagine them not hiring you. I'm attaching the application. And putting in a good word for you."

And then the xoxo that was always her goodbye.

Followed by the attachment, the application.

An application for a girl to get a job she couldn't have dreamed of ten years ago, a job with a salary containing bigger numbers than she's ever known in her life. A job for which she'd be "perfect."

Which is where Joannah and I part ways in our opinions. *I can't imagine them not hiring you.* Well, I can. Because the girl with no college degree, without even a high school degree if we're going to get technical (and I have a suspicion that they're going to get technical), who's lived in a sum total of two cities her entire life, without any marketing experience to her name— that's probably not the person they have in mind.

But what have I got to lose?
I click the link.

CHAPTER 10

*E*lectrician called, check.

Southern Electric, check.

No drippy murder candles needed (until it's open for Halloween), check.

YouTube channel set up (with Becca's help), check.

First video posted, check.

Sledgehammer purchased, check.

Crowbar purchased, check.

Conversations about Jackson mostly avoided, check.

But today he's coming to measure the kitchen while I do the tear out. I've got my very oldest jeans on, nasty tennis shoes, shirt with a tear in the armpit. I do NOT look like the model on the advertisement at the home repair store. I don't look like a model for anything except maybe Country Bill's Trailer and Hitch ("come on in for the lowest price possible"). But I do look like someone ready to tear a kitchen out.

When I text my friends the picture of the sledge-hammer, Macie hashtags it #murderhousestrikesagain.

Which reminds me to take a 'before' video of the kitchen. I move in a half circle, taking in the old cupboards stained with decades of grease and use, the cracking linoleum, even the ceiling decorated with the splatters of who knows what kinds of food.

"For real, be careful with that sledgehammer," Macie texts as I'm finishing the video.

And, well, it's solid advice. Especially since it's been a few years since I've used one. In fact, the last time was when I was a teenager and Mama begged me to knock out the back steps for her. They were broken concrete, cracks streaking through the centers, making them lopsided for Mama. I'd asked her who was going to come put in new steps so she could get out the back. "Ain't got no need for that," she said.

"Then what good's it do you for me to knock these out?" I asked.

"Just do it, Bobbi," she'd said, using her nickname for me.

"Only if you tell me who's gonna come fix it."

"I'll call Charlie if I has to," she'd said.

So I'd knocked them out. And naturally she'd never called my uncle Charlie. But it hadn't mattered since she'd spent most of her time in bed or on the couch or sometimes going out front for the mail. And then, before another year had rolled around, she was gone. Not just dead. But *gone*. Trailer sold, debts paid off, my own stuff packed into a singular suitcase. And that was that.

Rousing myself from the memory, I heft the sledgehammer. I got the smallest one I could. Twenty-five pounds. And it's not so bad. I take a swing through the air, feeling a little heat in my muscles. Not bad at all. Another swing, this time at the cupboard I'm knocking down. It cracks right down the center, half of it hanging, the other bit falling to the floor. Way easier than Mama's concrete.

In fact, it's probably best to switch to the crowbar and save the sledgehammer for the wall, or any bits I can't seem to get.

By the time Jackson arrives, I'm sitting in a pile of splinters, dust, and destruction. My shoulder muscles are burning mercilessly, and I'm taking a break, swigging from my water bottle.

"Well, look at that," Jackson says, with his deep drawl. "When the lady says she's gonna get 'er done, she's gonna get 'er done."

I nod, still chugging water, wishing I'd brought a couple of granola bars as well.

He pulls out his measuring tape and gets to work. I only have a few cupboards left. My mass destruction has released several roaches into the wild. And it's good I grew up like I did, or that would have made me lose it completely.

"You know a good pest company?" I ask, as one of the stragglers scampers its way underneath the crooked baseboards.

"I know a couple," he answers. "What you needing done?"

"This place has a ton of roaches," I answer. "Maybe not south Florida level, but a long way off from beautiful restoration level."

He nods. "Cheapest is going to be Ernest and Sons."

I take a final sip of water. It's almost gone now.

And I just have two more cupboards, but I find that I feel a little shy about ripping them off in front of Jackson. Like a girl playing at a job.

But after he's measured the southern wall, he glances at me. "Well, go on. Don't let me keep a lady from her work."

I put my work gloves back on, pick up the crowbar, then fit it in behind the cupboard, and jerk.

It's then that I realize why I felt shy about it. I look ridiculous. With my smallish frame, I'd been throwing all my weight against the crowbar, grunting and pushing. Alone, it felt empowering; now it feels goofy.

The second-to-last cupboard creaks away from the wall, splintering with bits of drywall dust floating into the air. I jerk and thrust again. And out it comes, collapsing into the heap with its brother cupboards.

"One to go," he says.

"One to go." But it's right by the corner where he's measuring. "Don't want to get in your way," I say.

"Ah, no, you're good," he answers, scooting over so I can get it. He's jotting measurements into that same little notebook he used for the estimate, not looking at me. I take my place by the final cupboard, jam the crowbar in, and brace my body. Jerk and pull. The cupboard moans. But it doesn't come off.

I grunt and jerk some more. Even though Jackson isn't watching me, I can feel him watching me—maybe not with his eyes, but with his ears, with his body.

"You want some help?" he asks.

"I think I've got it," I say as a portion of it cracks and breaks loose, but the stubborn corner bit is still there. "Urg," I grumble.

Jackson holds out a hand.

"No, it's okay," I say. "We agreed that I would do the tear out."

"And you have," he says. "I've got a little height, which might make it easier."

A little height, and a lot of muscle. Grudgingly, I look at the crowbar, then back up at him. I hand it over, feeling the pink rise in my cheeks. But when he fits it in, it doesn't budge for him either.

We both step back, inspecting it. He looks at the crowbar, then glances at the sledgehammer on the floor. "We can always fix the wall later," he says with a sly grin.

"Let's give it one more go without it," I say. "Maybe if we pull on it together."

We both grip it, hand over hand, shoulder to

shoulder, positioning our legs to give us the best pull. I like the feel of it, him beside me.

"On three," I say.

One huge jerk later, the cupboard splinters, the dust rises, a small army of brown roaches scampers to safety, but only the slimmest bit of cupboard breaks off, crashing to its grave.

"Sledgehammer it is," I say, wiping the sweat off my face.

Jackson is over by the cupboard, inspecting a black line peeking out from behind it.

"What is that?" I ask. "Paint? Please don't tell me it's mold."

"Not mold," he says, laughing, then stepping back.

I see the slight glint, like it's metal. I squint, step closer, touch it. "A safe?" I ask.

"Looks like it," he replies.

"Murder house strikes again," I murmur, reaching for the phone in my pocket to take a video. "When will we find the creepy hidden library with the revolving wall?"

"You mean you haven't knocked out all the walls yet," he says.

We both laugh. Then he asks, "You think anything's in the safe?"

"Couple of dust bunnies and a family of roaches," I respond with a smile.

"Maybe," he says. "Or maybe not. Don't suppose your memaw's will came with a combination."

"You'd not suppose correctly," I say, wondering how good Tad would be with breaking into an old safe. Aren't safecrackers supposed to see and feel the clicks somehow?

"Well," Jackson adds. "Turns out I know a guy."

"Why am I not surprised?" I ask.

"He ain't from here though."

"That's probably for the best," I say.

"Probably," he agrees. "Don't want too many rumors to fly. And I hope you checked your memaw's sock drawers. Never know where that woman went hiding her money."

"Yeah," I say, "all that money."

"You never know," he replies. "Country people like their stashes."

"Still not sure I've got the stamina to go through all Memaw's old pantyhose."

"It's got to be done some time," he answers.

"I suppose it does," I reply, looking through the doorway to the living room with the ancient, broken things.

"Your water's all gone," he says when I've cleared away as much wood as I can and loaded it into the trailer.

I nod. "Yeah, I'll have to bring more next time. I don't want to turn the water line back on until I have a plumber inspect the pipes."

"Smart," he says. "Better go grab you something before the dump."

"Can't," I answer. "They close at three, and I'm already pushing it."

He tips his chin up. "Got her loaded up tight?"

"Yup." I swing into my SUV, feeling a little like I'm hopping onto my horse and pulling a wagon along behind me. It's not a bad feeling if I'm honest —the sense of accomplishment—those cupboards were definitely the hardest of the work I'll have to do. And the secret safe was a fun find too, even though it's hard to believe there's anything in there at all.

When I get back, Jackson's still there, which surprises me. He's sitting on the porch swing with a couple of glasses of lemonade and a few sandwiches wrapped up in plastic.

"Thought I better bring you something to eat before you have to drive home," he says, simple as that.

And then I do something that seems insane. I tear up. If you'd asked me what might make me cry in this whole home renovation, I definitely wouldn't have told you a random guy with a couple of sandwiches. It just seems like completely the absolute wrong reaction.

I bat the tears back as hard as I can, trying to cover them with a laugh. "Wow," I say. "That is so nice."

He takes a few napkins out of the little bag he's packed, then pats the spot on the porch swing beside him. "Dig in."

I go for the lemonade first. I really am thirsty. But as I guzzle it, I barely register the taste. After all, I still need to get the plumber out here next. Then the pest guy. Or should that come first? At some point I'll need to pick out flooring. And there's that wall to get down.

I stop in the whirlwind of thought and look at Jackson, who's slowly unwrapping his sandwich and looking at me. "Penny for your thoughts?" he says.

"Not sure they're worth that much," I answer. "They're churning around like some kind of hurricane. I need to catch them and figure out what to do next with this old house."

"Maybe you really need to give them room to swirl," he says. "Let them die down on their own. The important things will still be there, and you'll be able to see them a lot more clearly."

"Maybe," I say, but I'm skeptical. Those thoughts are keeping me up at night. "I just want to get some decisions made. And soon."

"And you will," he says. "But at the very least, just let them go while you eat." He passes me a napkin, refills my empty glass from a thermos.

I pause to look at the drink, actual bits of pulp floating through the nectar. "Did you make this?" I ask.

He does a non-committal shrug thing and I notice the sandwiches next. He's tucked bacon, lettuce, and tomatoes that look dark red and home grown into a nutty wheat bread. I haven't had a thing since breakfast and I'm not sure anything has ever tasted so good.

The tears come at me again, trying to break

through. I take another gulp of lemonade to hold them back. "This is the best thing I've tasted, maybe ever," I say. "Thank you so much." I don't dare look at him for fear I'll start crying. I really do need to get my blood sugar up or something. My moods are starting to go haywire.

"No problem. Figured you'd be hungry, working like that all day. All I did was measure and watch you, and *that* made me hungry."

I laugh. "So you must not live far from here," I say.

"Not too far. I have a little house down the road. Closer to town, so I can get there when I need, but not too close to town. I still like to enjoy me a little country."

"Pretty sure everything around here is a *little* country."

"Guilty as charged," he says. "My house sits on a fat wooded acre. Wouldn't have it any other way."

"Sounds beautiful," I say. "And the tomatoes? Did you grow them?"

"Mama did," he says. "These are the last of the season. She picks them all this time of year and then pawns them off on any poor soul who will take them. Just like I'm doing to you right now."

"Mmmm," I say. "Anytime. I'm your girl. Just give the excess to me."

"Agreed," he drawls.

"So how often do you, um, get jobs?" I ask, curious about how this man stays afloat.

"This type of work?" he answers. "A few times a week when I have time. Speaking of," he says, changing the subject. "I called my safe-cracking friend when you were at the dump. He says he has an opening tomorrow."

Sunday. The final day of my weekend and I'd have to spend it down here. All to see if the safe is just full of dust. But what else can I do? I'm not sure how much you should trust "safe-cracking friends" without supervision.

"I can meet you here at eleven with my friend, if that's not too early," he says. "Then maybe after…" he begins.

I interrupt without realizing it, my brain barreling forward like it does. "Eleven is perfect," I say. "That way I'll have a little time back home to relax before Monday hits and it's back to work." I stop, realize he had started to say something. "I'm sorry. I interrupted. What were you saying?"

"Ah, nothing," he answers, leaning back against the porch swing. "And what is *work*?"

"Well, nothing like this kind of work," I say. "I work, um, at a department store up in Swallowsville."

"Swanky," he says, trying to get rid of his Kentucky accent and not succeeding.

I giggle. "Not sure about swanky," I say. "But it pays the bills, and then some. And I enjoy it—helping people find what they need."

"And then whacking out interiors on the weekends," he says.

"Well, not most weekends," I answer.

"You've still got that wall to go," he teases.

"Don't remind me. I think I can probably come again in a couple weekends." I pause. "Or maybe since I'll be down here tomorrow, I should do it then. But then there goes the whole Sunday." I sigh. I really don't want to, but how else is this house going to get done?

"You remind me of my sister," he says. "Tough as nails. Though you wouldn't have guessed it because she was tiny like you."

"She live around here?"

He casts a sideways glance at me. "Not anymore."

"Move to the city just like me?" I ask, laughing.

"Only if the pearly gates count as a city," he says,

smiling. "She passed a few years ago. Boating accident."

I nearly choke on my sandwich. "Oh, Jackson. I'm so sorry. I didn't mean to—"

"I said a thing and you asked a natural question," he replies. "Don't apologize. Besides, I like to talk about her. She was a flame when she was here and now she's a piece of sun in my memory."

He utters this little slip of poetry without a pause or a drop of irony. There's nothing for me to do but nod.

"And your family?" he asks. "Gone too, I take it, since you're the one with the old family house."

Another nod, my throat feeling tight, but not—like Jackson said because of those sunshine memories—more because of my lack of sunshine, and sometimes lack of memories. Sure, I've got plenty of memories with Mama, and sure, some of those were even good. But watching Daddy destroy himself and then Mama destroy herself in another way. Never knowing Memaw, and not even knowing who my grandpa was, well, it's enough to choke anyone up.

"You the only child?" he asks.

"Yup," I say.

"Welp, now I am too." He kind of bumps my shoulder and I kind of like it. "You know what they say about how spoiled only children are. Sounds like us, don't it?"

"Sure does," I answer. "I mean, look at us. Living in the lap of luxury like this."

We both laugh—clothes dirty, trailer still hitched to my SUV, dust barely settled inside the house.

The sun is just beginning to set—the days shortening in leaps and bounds now as we head toward fall. "September's almost over," I say, looking at the oranges and pinks that spread over the hills.

"Gorgeous, isn't it?"

The grasses capture the golds from the sky, and everything lights up just as the frogs begin to sing.

"It is," I murmur. With the softest movement ever, he nudges the swing back, tipping us into a gentle sway. Rocking. Back and forth. Like babies. Like comfort. Like safety. Like love. I have a nearly uncontrollable urge to lean my head on his shoulder, as though it's exactly where my head should have been my entire life.

I jam my foot down, stopping us.

Country, I tell myself. He's a nice man, an incredibly good-looking, nice man. Maybe he wasn't even the cliché type of guy I'd pegged him as at first, but no matter what, he's one hundred percent country— the flannel, the truck, the part-time, fix-it sort of job.

"I'd better get going," I say, wrapping up the remaining crumbs into the napkin, then swallowing any final droplets of lemonade.

"Watch for deer," he says, standing up with me. And then, like some type of magician, he produces a fresh water bottle. "For the road," he says.

It would be ridiculous to say that it's the nicest thing anyone has ever done for me, but it's definitely one of the nicest things anyone has ever done for me. Which feels a little sad when I think about it. I look at the bottle stupidly—just a generic bottle of water. But I was so thirsty, and I'd worked so hard all day, and he thought about me, about what I might be feeling, what I might be needing. Other than Macie and Becca, precious few people in my life have ever done that.

I want to hug him. Instead, I stick out my hand for him to shake. He shakes it, his hand calloused, but warm at the center, rough fingers, soft grip.

"Thank you, Jackson," I say.

"See you tomorrow, Fireball," he says. "Hopefully, as a newly minted millionaire when Jim gets that safe open."

"Yeah," I say. "Let's count on that."

CHAPTER 11

I don't count on it.

I don't count on it so much that I don't bother to text Macie and Becca about the safe.

I feel a little guilty about that when the safe-cracker shows up—no Kentucky in his accent at all—with several strange instruments as well as a few picks that look a lot like knives. #murderhousestrikesagain

I take out my phone to video and he sort of shakes his head.

Obediently, I tuck the phone away, not asking questions. I'm glad that Jackson is here and find myself taking a step closer to him.

The guy—Jim—uses a stethoscope, just like on TV,

but he doesn't only listen for the clicks. He uses the knife-like things to jiggle and jangle, and with all that sharp equipment, I'm once again glad that Jackson is here, joshing with this guy, and keeping me from being murdered and robbed. Although there's not going to be anything at all to rob, I remind myself. Because the safe, I'm sure, is just full of dead bugs and dead air.

Except that when he finally gets it open, it's not.

Inside are several wooden boxes engraved with birds and vines. To be honest, I would have been thrilled enough just to find those. But inside the boxes we discover several gold necklaces, a vintage diamond ring—pear shaped—with two broken prongs and a bent band. We also find nearly four thousand dollars.

The money sits in a little wad, as though bits just got shoved in from time to time, before the cupboard got put in—a five here, a twenty there. It's not going to pay for my retirement, but it might, in fact, pay for flooring.

Jackson whistles. Jim grins.

"How much do I owe you?" I ask.

"I usually charge ten percent of what's in the safe, but I owe Jackson a favor or two, so don't worry about it."

I look back and forth between the two of them. "No, really," I say. "I'm happy to pay."

"To keep it on the up and up, you can just pass me couple of those twenty dollar bills," he says. "That's more than enough for my time and my gas." He puts his tiny, sharp instruments into their felt cases. "Pleasure was mine."

Then he climbs into his Toyota Camry with its New Jersey plates, and he's off.

"Where on earth did you meet him?" I ask when the dust from his car has settled.

"Military," Jackson answers.

I guess that tracks. "But he's not from around here," I say.

"He's not from around anywhere," Jackson answers. "He goes where he's called to go, and that's a lot of places."

"Government work?" I ask.

"Sometimes," Jackson answers, with a sly grin.

"Well," I say, glancing back at the money. "I guess *this* calls for a celebration. Can I take you to lunch? I would have invited Jim too," I say quickly, trying to make it sound as little like a date as possible. "But he ran off too fast."

"Well, I never could say 'no' to a lady," Jackson answers, with a little bow.

"Anything good around here?" I ask, glancing down at my phone.

"Well, you know, we've got a real nice McDonald's."

I glance up sharply, relieved to see that he's smiling.

"Sounds like a good start," I say.

"We only do the finest in Midvale," he answers with a grin.

"Obviously."

"We've also got a pizza joint. Barbeque and bar."

"Chili's?" I ask, fishing for something a teeny bit nicer.

"I knew you were swanky," he says, laying his accent on especially thick for effect. "But also no," he says. "There's a pretty little pasta place called Milan's. That's probably as fancy as it gets. Meaning, that's where all the teens go for prom."

"Sounds like just the place," I answer. "We can take my car."

"It's not even hitched up," he says.

"Swanky," I answer.

"Exactly," he says. "You ought to put on some of that jewelry too. Bling it up, as the kids say."

"Do they say that?" I ask.

"I have no idea," he laughs. "But seriously, grab a

necklace or that ring. If you're going to celebrate, might as well do it in style."

"Maybe they'll turn my skin green," I say.

"Doubt it," he replies, looking at the open jewelry boxes. "Bet these things have a story, especially that one." He points to the bent ring.

"No doubt," I say. "But I'm not sure it's a happy one." I pick it up, feeling the weight of the large diamond—if it's a diamond at all, and not a cubic zirconia or something. It's got to be at least a carat, which seems unfathomable for a family like mine. I run my fingers against the sharp points of the broken prongs and then let them slip along the bent band. I know that shape—like the wearer hit something hard while it was on. Mama had rings like that —all bent out of shape because when she got mad, she'd go around hitting everything from the wall to the door to the countertop.

"Did you know your grandfather?" he asks.

"Not at all," I answer, not including the fact that I didn't know my memaw either. I might have had a foggy memory or two of a woman with a gray knot on her head, peering at me from the kitchen window like Mama used to, the smell of bacon and grits. But maybe those were just made up.

Tucking the ring back into the box and shutting it, I say, "Anyway, we better be off."

Only just then my phone rings. It's Jamie from work. "Just a sec," I say to Jackson, locking up the house and taking the call.

Jamie sounds like she ate hot coals for breakfast, her voice so hoarse, I can barely hear her. "Hey, Gretchen. I know it's your day off, but I woke up feeling like death."

"You sound like it too," I say.

"Any chance you could switch me tonight for another day this week."

"Of course," I answer, though from the sound of it, she might be out for longer than that. "Remind me what time you start. I'm not at home right now."

"Three," she says. "I know it's last minute. I just… this morning I went back to bed, thinking that would do the trick, but I just woke up and I think I feel even worse."

"Don't worry about a thing," I say, glancing at Jackson, feeling a little twist in the pit of my stomach. "Call Joannah and tell her I'm coming in for you."

"I owe you," Jamie says.

"Just get some rest and don't worry," I say.

Jackson is standing at the bottom of the porch steps. As far as I know, there's no way he could have known what went on in my phone conversation, but when I walk slowly down to him, he says, "Change of plans?"

"I'm really sorry."

"Someone called?" he asks.

"Friend from work. She's sick. Needs me to take her shift."

"You better go back and get that jewelry and money then," he says. "No saying how safe it'll be in this old house."

I nod, turning back to the porch. "I'm really sorry," I repeat. Then, "Look. Why don't you go and treat yourself? I've taken so much of your time this morning. At least let me pay you." I open my purse, pulling out a couple of twenties. "Here."

He's smiling still, but it feels just a little forced. He steps toward me. "Keep your money," he says, gently folding my fingers over the bills. "I'll take a raincheck instead."

I nod, not quite sure what I'm agreeing to, hyper-aware of the heat of his hand over mine. Then he breaks away, and I hurry into the house for the cash and the bent jewelry with its stories I don't know and never will.

CHAPTER 12

On Monday morning, I go to the bank and the jeweler before mentioning a word to my friends about the safe. The money's real—that's easy to tell. I'm about to deposit it in my regular old savings account when my traitor of a mouth opens up and says, "How much does it cost to open a business account?"

"Just seventy-five dollars," the woman replies. "Is that something you'd like to do today?"

And then before my brain can stop me, my mouth says, "Actually, yes. Are there any other hidden fees?"

"No," she says. "But you can head on in to talk to Tim." She gestures to a little room to the side. "He'll be able to answer your questions and give you any details you need."

I walk to the room, my feet pulling me, while my brain is who knows where—maybe back in murderhouse.

By the time I'm driving to the jewelers, I'm the proud owner of a new business account, with a pamphlet in my pocket about how to register for an LLC.

I've got three necklaces, one with a ruby and freshwater pearl, one a long gold chain, and one a string of pearls. Plus the ring.

The jeweler is leaning over the counter, magnifying glass in hand. "You'd have to have them properly appraised to get the real value. An appraisal usually costs about a hundred dollars apiece, though maybe we could do it a little cheaper for all four. But I can tell you that for most of them an appraisal probably isn't worth it. Like this piece," she says, holding up the one with the ruby and pearl. "It looks like gold fill. There's no stamp designating it with a carat such as 14K, and real gold always has a stamp."

"So it's gold plate?" I say.

"Not exactly," she replies. "Gold fill is a mixture of gold and brass. It's usually about 5% gold whereas plate is almost none at all. And it's clearly an older, vintage piece, which might give it a little more resale value." Her voice drifts off as though to say, *but not a lot...*

"And the gems?" I ask.

"Oh, they're real," she says. "But the ruby is so small that it won't be worth much and the freshwater pearl, well, same thing. Super cool piece though. It's just that back in the day they didn't have as much money, so sometimes something made with gold fill *was* fine jewelry. For normal folks of course."

I lean over the counter, looking at it. It's definitely a cool piece, a nearly worthless cool piece of vintage jewelry. "Not much hope for the other pieces then," I say.

"Oh, don't be too hasty," she replies. "This chain has the stamp. See." She hands me the magnifying glass and shows me a little engraved stamp near the clasp of the chain. 10K. "Not worth millions, but you could get several hundred for that since it's a twenty-inch chain. And this..." She holds up the string of pearls, admiring it for a moment. "Any idea how old it is?"

"Not really," I say. "It was my Me—my grandma's, and I assume that it was from her younger years."

"Family heirloom?"

"Maybe."

That pang again, from not knowing anything about this woman whose house and things I now call my own.

"It looks old," she says. "These days pearls aren't worth as much as they used to be because they can, uh, farm them."

"Yes, cultured pearls," I say. "But those are still valuable, right?"

"Ah, that's the million dollar question," she says. "Pun entirely intended."

I laugh.

"Cultured pearls still have some value—they're still real pearls after all. But if they were old enough, then they might be considered 'wild' or 'natural' pearls. And if they were their value would be enormous. Was your family rich?" she asks.

I kind of snort. "No."

"Like most families," she says, with a smile that I like.

"Which means they're probably cultured, which

means the value is probably average. Maybe a few hundred bucks. Cultured pearls aren't too hard to come by these days. But this piece is set on silk thread with tiny knots between to keep the pearls from rubbing or breaking. And the clasp is real gold. 14K."

"And if I wanted to find out if they were, um, wild?"

"You'd have to have them X-rayed by a gemological library. Which I would only do if you're pretty confident about their age because it's not cheap."

"I imagine."

"Which leaves us," she says. "With this piece." She fingers the ring, turning it all directions. "I think it calls for the microscope."

"Is it a real microscope?" I ask, looking at the thing that looks just like what you'd use in a high school biology class.

"Yes," she says. "We usually just use these for a full appraisal, but…"

"You're having too much fun."

"You know, I kind of am," she says, laughing. "These old pieces are just so cool." She straightens her suit. "Though seriously, I can't give you an offi-cial appraisal without some money exchanging hands." She puts on her best serious face, and then smiles again. "Now let's look at this little mama."

The name she gives it feels too appropriate, though the diamond is not little and as far as I know, the ring was gifted before anyone was a mama, though in deep Kentucky, who knows? I have to admit I'm surprised (and suspicious) at the size of the ring. It is big, probably a little over a carat. And the gold looks real to me. Not that I'm a jeweler, but I AM pretty good at noticing how things look.

She turns it around under the microscope, cooing and clucking.

"So it's real?" I say, assuming a piece of plastic would have been a quick glance.

"Real and beautiful," she says. "It's not quite fit for the Smithsonian or anything, but it's quite clear with very few inclusions, and the cut is nice, allowing the light to shine through, which is what gives diamonds that sparkle. Plus, the band is 18K, which explains the bend here."

It doesn't even begin to explain the bend. Not really. Even if it is easier to damage a soft 18-carat band.

"Wonder what happened?" she says.

"Probably got hit on something," I say.

She looks at me for a second, then says, "We can

fix the band for you for fairly cheap. I'd bet it would fit you." She glances at my hands.

"Um," I say. "Not right now. Not a diamond ring."

"Well, we're here for you if you ever need us. We can fix the band for about $100 and give you a true appraisal with paperwork for about the same."

"And—not a real appraisal of course—but what would you estimate the value to be?"

"I mean, you're looking at least $4000-5000."

I kind of choke on my gasp. "Really?" I ask.

"Really," she says.

"So I could sell that thing and—"

"You'd sell it?" she asks. "Wasn't it your grandmother's?"

My *memaw's*, I think, like the name is a correction. "I meant, just as a thought." I clear my throat.

She nods, but I can tell it's just to be professional. It's easy to see that she wants to ask a bunch of questions.

"We weren't close," I say, trying to clear the air, but making it feel thicker.

She nods again.

"Thank you for all your help. You've been amazing. I'm sure I'll be back."

"Ask for Andrea," she says, pointing to herself. "And, I probably shouldn't say this, because I'm so professional and all, but think about it before you sell your grandmother's ring. At least dig up its story first."

"Thank you," I say. "I will."

If I can, that is. If I can.

CHAPTER 13

"You're never going to believe this," I say to my friends. Just like I did that first time on Memaw's property.

"What has murder house done now?" Macie asks. We're standing at a little outdoor café near the park. And I can feel it—the chill in the air.

"Murder house has granted me about $8,000."

"You're kidding," Macie says, taking her hibiscus tea from the barista. Becca's already got her hot chocolate and is blowing over the top like a kid. We walk to a bench at the park and in the shade, it's even cooler. Supposedly it's going to dive into freezing next week, just as September turns over to October. We might even get some flurries—almost unheard of at this time of year in Kentucky. For now, we're trying to enjoy autumn as autumn.

"Nope, not kidding." I set my laptop on the table, ignoring my coffee. Truthfully, I feel so jittery already that I probably should have taken a page from Macie's book and gotten myself a nice, calming tea. "We found this safe when I was knocking out the kitchen."

"Who's 'we?'" Becca asks, though her little eyebrow pop seems to say she has a decent idea.

"That guy. The handyman."

"*That guy,*" Becca says with air quotes.

"Hand-y man," Macie snickers.

"Are you a ten-year-old boy?" I ask. "I thought you were the responsible one."

"Nope," Macie says. "That's Becca now."

"The *repair* man," I say. "Anyway, *I* found this safe. And he knew a guy who cracks safes."

"Murder house," Macie whispers.

"It definitely felt that way. But this safecracker guy got it open and I thought it'd be empty, but it wasn't."

"To the tune of $8000?" Macie asks.

"To the tune of $4000 and some old jewelry, most notably a diamond ring."

"That house is the wildest place," Becca says.

"It *is* a little wild," I answer, thoughtfully.

"And there wasn't, like, a booby trap or something?" Macie asks.

"Not unless I've developed a curse of some type," I say.

Macie leans over like she's inspecting me. "A little flushed," she says. Then, "Hand-y man."

"Time to be serious, ladies," I say, sipping my coffee to warm up a bit. Maybe we should have gotten a seat inside the cafe.

I open my laptop. "Let's get that Kickstarter account going."

<hr>

We set up eight tiers.

Book club: $200 (finger foods served)

Hayride: $300 (hot cider served)

Girl's night: $500 (drinks or coffees plus book-themed snacks, free lip gloss)

Murder Mystery Night: $1000 (dinner)

Girl's overnight: $2000 (drinks, breakfast served, free lipstick)

Romantic overnight: $2500 (wine, breakfast in bed)

Wedding reception: $5000, plus catering costs
Wedding reception, dinner included: $8,000

It feels pricey to me. Like, no one spends $200 to have a book club at an old farmhouse, but Becca assures me that this is how they work. A little expensive, but with fun extra perks.

"And you're going to make it amazing," Becca says. "The décor, the furniture. People are going to be paying for the vibe as much as anything."

I do appreciate a good vibe and my imagination is soaring with how I would design the interior, what I would do with the gardens outside, and how much all of that would cost of course. I'm penciling in numbers with random-ish estimates. I'll make a few trips to the home store and the furniture store. But, with my estimate—new bathrooms, paint, carpet, a little landscaping, a whole house of new furniture—pretty stuff—plus food for the events, I'm going to need to earn $60,000-$80,000. I set my pencil to the side, toss it if I'm honest.

Staggering, overwhelming numbers.

Which is why I'm confused when Becca tells me to set the lowest goal for $10,000.

"That won't be enough," I tell her.

"It doesn't have to be," she says. "But if you set it too high and then don't make it, you won't get any money. That's how it works."

"But if I set it too low and don't get *enough* money...?" I say. "How will I design and furnish it? That's a whole lot of lipstick to sell on the side."

"Which you are excellent at selling," Becca says. "But seriously, don't worry. You'll get people signing up. You're magic at that."

I rub my head, retrieve my pencil from the edge of the table.

We set it to go live in a few weeks. Becca wanted it to be sooner, but I'm working almost constantly over the next few weeks, and just need some time to concentrate on that, and to catch my breath from this.

I pencil a few more names of people into my notebook—connections I can invite to see the Kickstarter. I've got several hundred Facebook friends and I'll send a personal email to my work friends and my lipstick sellers. I tap my fingers. "Anybody else?"

"Definitely send one to Tad," Macie replies.

"And me," Becca adds.

I love them. So much.

But it still doesn't feel like it'll be enough money.

My phone dings with an email notification as soon as I get to my car.

Dear Ms. Stephens,

We've received your application and references and would like to set up an introductory interview. Below you'll find the times we have available. Please click one to sign up. All interviews will be held at our office in Louisville. We look forward to meeting you.

Sincerely,

Jane Matthews, HR

. . .

here are three times available for interviews. All during the week. I'm going to have to take a day off if I decide to do the interview. Which I realize, my finger hovering over one of the times, I'm going to. It's a shot in a million, but why not?

What's weird is that I'm a little relieved that none are on Saturday—on the one day I was planning to go to the house.

CHAPTER 14

INTERLUDE: JACKSON

I drive past Gretchen's farmhouse on the way to work. And, for the record, I don't have to. It costs me an extra eight minutes to take the road to her house, to crane my neck trying to see if her car is in the drive. Like I'm sixteen again with my first real crush.

Not that crushes usually work out.

I wonder if Gretchen's rain check will actually happen—it's been a couple weeks since she came here. So maybe once the euphoria of the safe wore off, so did her enthusiasm for me. Although enthusiasm seems like a strong word. She tolerates me, maybe even treats me like some sort of pleasant brotherly figure—comfortable, even trusting, but not much more. And why?

I swing around onto a country road and head into town.

Distance maybe. Although this is her home, and who wouldn't want to return home?

It's a thought I sit on for a while, turning the hot air in my car to cold, letting it chill me for the last two minutes of my drive. I count out the seconds, hating every one, but the rush of cold always gives me a mini adrenaline boost, which helps me with the long hospital shifts. I can't go in warm and cozy or I'll never make it through.

I step out of my car and into the frigid air. No coat, just my scrubs.

I've only got two twelve-hour shifts this week, which will give me more time to work on the house. Once Gretchen gets the cupboards delivered and the wall out, I'm going to find myself with a lot to do.

The side hustle is like my creative outlet. The yin to the yang of my work at the ER. My dad spent his life building things. He wanted me to follow, taking over his carpentry business, but I never was quite as good as he was—at business or carpentry—and after my sister Essie died, I didn't have the heart to work day in and day out at the business.

I *did* keep his little shop in the basement, occasionally making something here or there. When a neighbor needed help with his drywall and offered to pay, my side job began. I loved re-creating a room —the more drastic, the better. Maybe that was what I loved so much about Gretchen's farmhouse. All the old, classic details and features, but also all the new potential.

I'd managed to talk Gretchen into keeping the original wood crown molding. It hadn't been hard. She had an eye for beauty and—I had a feeling—a decent sense for business. And I had a keen sense of how to build a room so it would look the best.

It wasn't quite carpentry, but it filled a void. A void that the fast, brutal pace of being an ER nurse didn't.

Yeah, sure, sure, I loved my job, or I used to. Helping people who were in desperate need, doing my best to keep them stable, to give them a second shot at living—it had felt so powerful. But with nursing shortages all over the country, it was twelve hours of running from patient to patient. And, in the ER, we only got two types of patient— critical, or didn't-need-to-be-there—each type stressful in their own way. Add to that the fact that the other nurses and techs and doctors were as grumpy and tired as I was. By the end of every shift, I was always more than ready to settle in with some wood or paint or even a sheet of drywall.

Mama gave me plenty of chances with her old house, and neighbors were always needing a little help. I, however, didn't have a keen sense for business, and was always giving things away for cheap or free.

My phone dings as I'm about to walk into the hospital. "You free today?" Gretchen asks.

I sigh. Nope. "What are you needing?" I ask.

"Finally got a day off work. Planning to take that wall down, and hoping the materials for the kitchen will arrive. Wanted to talk it through with you."

I wish she wanted to talk more than that through with me. I think of her laughter when we got the safe open, the way she turned that ring over and over in her hand. It had definitely been a surprise, her memaw's ring. In fact, it seems like the whole house is a surprise for her. And why? She's the only one left. I feel a pang for her about that. A pang and a bit of suspicion—her living up in Swallowsville, working at a nice store, trying to make everything pretty.

I'd asked Mama about her memaw. "That woman kept to herself," Mama said. "Life had disappointed her."

Which is maybe the same type of thing that had driven Gretchen into the city—into the new life she'd created for herself.

"I won't be available until after eight," I text. "And I know that's late for you."

"A little," she replies. "I'll leave the plans on the counter. Hopefully when you come by, the wall will be gone."

"You know how to do it?" I ask. "You don't want to hit any wires or anything."

"I watched a YouTube tutorial."

"Maybe I can come check on you over my lunch break," I say. Not that I'm likely to get one. I hear a siren approaching, and step into the hospital, ready for my shift.

"I'll be fine," she answers. Then, after a second. "But thank you."

CHAPTER 15

The wall comes down in a satisfying crash of dust and wood. Well, not all at once. But several crashes, several pieces, lots of sweat.

And when I can see through the wreckage into the front room, I break into tears. Like the world just opened up. Like I just created something that wasn't there.

It feels good. Especially after the tautness from the stress of working more than full time—six and a half days a week for the last couple weeks, with Jamie sick, and my regular shift. Plus these renovations, plus overextending myself financially and hoping for the best. I keep telling myself I've got $8000 in hand, in addition to my savings of a few thousand. And my Kickstarter of course. Which is going to kick start tomorrow at noon.

I'll be here. I'm too nervous to be watching it all day long. And the forecast is calling for snow later in the week. We rarely get snow in January, much less October, and I'm determined to be done with this round of house stuff before the snow hits.

It's the perfect excuse for dumping the Kick-starter off on Becca. She's happy to babysit it while I come down here. Especially since I told her Jackson would be working on the house as well.

Unfortunately for Becca and her little plot, while he's working, I'll be busy painting the kitchen, tearing out the remaining carpet, and calling people about the hardwood. If I have extra time (which seems unlikely), I still need to pick out at least three rooms of furniture. To be paid with by money I don't yet have.

So, yeah, it feels good to have a little cry.

Some parts happy satisfaction. Some parts worried hot mess.

I gather up the wood and chunks of dry wall and load them onto the trailer. A light rain is starting to fall, so I hurry in to leave the plans for Jackson on an old stool.

A stool that faces the wall that is no more.

I stare.

Through the gaping opening. To the room beyond, to the future beyond. I've caught glimpses of it already. But without that wall, it looks a little clearer. This room, full of people, laughing or talking or exchanging vows. A shiver runs down my spine. Or maybe that's just a chill from the old windows that need to be replaced.

I step through the frame of the wall that once was and walk into the living room, touching the crown molding, imagining the floors smooth and gleaming with polish.

I run a finger along one of the antique tables. It's all dinged up and dingy, the finish uneven and coated with something that might be from tobacco smoke. But it's got pretty little scalloping along the bottom and gorgeous legs. I think I've seen another just like it in one of the bedrooms. I could bring it down into this room, refinish them. Looking around, seeing the room in the new light, I wonder how many other things might be able to stay with a little makeover.

Because if there's one thing I'm good at, it's the perfect makeover.

I stop at the bookshelves. They're set into the wall. But with white paint, it would brighten up the entire room. A few vases, some classic leather bound books, and then another shelf with fun stuff for guests to read if they get bored.

The fireplace needs to be inspected. I add that to my mental list. I really want to get it functional. It's surrounded by slate that reflects different colors in the light. I can only imagine how gorgeous it would be with a fire inside. But the brick for the hearth needs to be replaced. Or maybe exchanged for more slate—that'll cost a pretty penny. And then something to brighten it as well—I'm not sure what.

"You're not going to knock that off as well, are you?" a voice says from the kitchen.

I whirl around to see Jackson standing behind my newly-destroyed wall, a long coat wrapped tight around him.

"Just checking to make sure you'd avoided the wires," he says.

I laugh, then take a bow. "Yes, thank you."

"Glad you're alive," he says, like he was really worried I wouldn't be. "And I think you should leave the slate."

"Planning to," I say. "Just not sure what to do to brighten it up."

"You could always add a mantle that matched the lighter tones within the slate. Then maybe use pieces of slate for some sort of décor or bookends to connect the motif."

And, you know, he's still got the accent, the absolute drawl, still got the hair tossed back, the nice biceps, but suddenly he doesn't feel quite so country. "That's a fantastic idea," I say, cocking my head to the side, imagining the magic of the colors. "Do you have a sec to go over the plans?"

"Not really, honestly," he says. "I've got to get back. I just wanted to be sure you were okay and I had a couple of minutes, so I rushed over."

"Oh," I say. I can't help but notice how pleased I was when he showed up and how disappointed I feel that he's going away. "You can grab them if you want and we can talk tomorrow."

"Sounds like a plan," he says with that sweet drawl. And then he's gone, leaving a chill from the too-early winter air in his wake.

I really can't remember a time when it's snowed in October.

Which makes it easy not to believe that it will.

CHAPTER 16

The first flakes begin to fall the next day as Jackson and I are going over the kitchen plans. The flakes are fat, motherly things that give birth to hundreds then thousands of chubby little children.

The roads were already slick from the icy rain that had fallen all night, freezing as the temperatures had dropped that morning, and coating the trees, power lines, and everything else in a thin sheet of ice. Like snow fairies had done the decorating. Snow fairies who didn't give a rat's behind if people had to skate to their mailboxes. If, in fact, the mail actually came.

"Tell me you had them turn the water on," Jackson says. "You don't want the pipes freezing."

"Yeah," I say. "Thank goodness. But the snow wasn't supposed to come until tomorrow."

Jackson shrugs, checking the boxes that contain the cupboards he's going to be installing today. "And the ice wasn't supposed to come until tonight."

"Good thing I brought snacks," I grumble, nodding to the box I've brought, which is fully stocked. Even a few hot chocolate packets, and mugs to go with them. I figured if I was going to spend a lot of time here today (and all winter), I might as well do it with a few creature comforts. Starting with pretty mugs.

"If only the house was ready for a winter party," I say. "This would be perfect."

"Is that what you're going to do with the old house?" Jackson asks with surprise. "Entertain?"

I realize that he probably assumed I was going to fix it and sell it. Because that would be the *logical* thing to do. I clear my throat. "Yeah, possibly."

"Interesting," he says, drawing out the word.

"Sounds a little nuts, huh? And, I mean, I still might sell it and stuff. But I was thinking—well my friend just got engaged and people are always needing, you know, reception halls and business meeting venues, and—you know—stuff. So I thought it might be kind of cool if this was just…"

"Ready for business," he finishes for me.

"Well, yeah."

"It's a cool idea," he says. "My mama will love it. She's already happy you're fixing it up because she says it'll be good for house values in the area."

"Yes, unless something goes horribly wrong," I explain.

At that moment both of us look outside. The snowflake children have grown and are now birthing snow grandbabies. It's honestly a little difficult to see through it to the yard beyond. Grass and trees are covered now and the snow is beginning to pile up on the road.

"Well, I'll be," Jackson says. "I'm not sure I believed them."

"I definitely didn't," I say. "Maybe I'll heat us some water for tea."

"You mean on the stove you don't have yet?" he asks.

"There's a microwave in one of the bedrooms," I answer.

We both pause to watch at the window, and it seems like in just minutes another half inch has accumulated.

"Actually, maybe you better head home," Jackson says.

I wave an arm. "Nope. This is my last day off for the next six days. I've got to take advantage of it."

He glances out the window at my car, narrowing his eyes at the tires.

"I just bought new ones a few months ago," I say.

"Snow tires?" he asks.

"New tires," I say, "With nice, deep grooves. I'll be fine."

He nods slowly. "Just make sure you're out of here in time to get home before dark."

"Okay, Granny," I say.

He tries to smile at the joke, but is still watching the snow.

"Come on," I say, snapping the papers to get his attention. "Let's get moving."

I drag a couple of chairs into the living room as well as a box of slate that I found in one of the outbuildings.

Jackson covers the windows in the kitchen with cardboard to protect them, then begins slicing open the boxes containing the cupboards.

While he sorts and organizes cupboard parts, I position the slate around the hearth, then make a few calls, trying to get a hold of someone who does tile. No one answers.

I sigh. At least the floor guys will be here next

week. Then we can really get moving with furniture. Though I should also be sure to have the paint done before the flooring starts. I make several frantic notes in my phone. I actually already bought the paint. I figured if I got desperate and no one could do it, then, well, I could myself.

In all my free time and stuff. Though, looking around, I figure I could probably even start today. At least get this room done.

I notice that Jackson has brought in a little pile of wood and placed it in the rack by the fireplace, along with a pack of matches that looks to be about seven hundred years old and a box of little wood chips, partially used, labeled 'firestarters.' I wonder where he found those. I haven't gotten the fireplace inspected yet, but the old furnace is chugging away, trying to catch up to the cold, and I figure there's no time like the present.

"What's going to happen if the fireplace is messed up?" I ask.

"A whole lot of smoke," Jackson says, hammering stuff between comments. "Especially with that wood. I found it in a pile out back, but it's all a little damp. Should be well seasoned though."

"Well-seasoned?" I ask.

"Old enough to burn," he answers.

"So, just smoke?" I ask.

"Yes," he says, coming to the wall hole and looking through at me. "But you'd have to then extinguish the fire somehow if it was smoking everywhere."

"Like, um, throw the wood outside?"

He smirks—a legitimate smirk. I didn't even really know what a smirk looked like until I saw his face. "Have you even checked to see if the flue is open?" he asks.

"Uh, yeah," I say. "The *flue.* I'll just tell Alexa to open it up."

"I thought you were raised country," he says.

I've absolutely never said such a thing. I've only ever said that I left when I was young and live in Swallowsville and work in a department store. But now I say, "I was raised trailer park country, Jackson. We didn't have flues."

"That's for the best in a trailer," he adds with no irony, but maybe just the tiniest hint of a smile. "See this thing," he says, stepping through the wall hole and making his way to the fireplace. It's a little knob by the fireplace. "You turn it to open and close the flue."

"And the flue is?" I ask.

Here he's a little stumped too. "The flue is where the smoke goes. You open it to let the smoke out, or close it to keep critters and leaves and stuff from coming in. I'm guessing it's closed since the house has been shut up for so long. No one wants birds—or worse, raccoons—setting up shop in your fireplace." He turns the knob, and something creaks. "Let's hope that works."

I nod, but don't move.

"You ever started a fire?" he asks.

I have. Years ago, in our yard outside the trailer. Daddy liked to burn trash and sometimes I would help him. It's something I'd forgotten, a memory that leaps up, that I only *just* catch in time before it slips away again. Even more surprising than the memory is that there's something sweet in it. Daddy wasn't yelling or cursing or drinking, just standing by the flames, our faces lit and warmed by the blaze, both of us quiet against the roar and heat of that thing that was even bigger than Daddy was.

"Nope," I say, shoving the memory away.

"Here," he says, holding out his hand for the box of matches.

"You think those will even work?" I ask.

"If they don't nothing else in here will," he says, still waiting for me to hand him the matches.

"It's okay," I say. "You're busy. I'll figure it out."

"It'll only take me a sec," he says, but I don't hand the matches over.

He smiles and steps away. "A lady who knows what she wants."

But am I?

I finger the matches. The sticks honestly look nearly moldy, but I strike one anyway, and it catches. For a moment I just watch the blaze, trying to remember. It nearly burns my fingers before I blow it out, shaking my head.

Time to build a fire.

I take the open box of fire starters. Little bits of tinder, probably with some sort of combustible on them. I make a little pile, stack a few small pieces of firewood on top. They're light and from somewhere in my memory, I know that's a good thing for starting fires. Then the bigger pieces. They're also a bit light, but a little damp just like Jackson said.

Every once in a while, I hear the sounds in the kitchen stop and I know Jackson is peeking at me through the wall hole.

I don't look back, just strike another match,

watch it for one final moment, thinking of the way Daddy would throw it on the fire. Of course, he'd already doused everything with gasoline, so it always lit with a little more sha-boom than mine does.

I hold the match under the edge of one of the fire starters. It blackens just a tinge before the flame touches my fingers and I drop it. Another match that doesn't light, then one that goes out before the fire starter catches. It's not till the fifth that I get the tiniest little flame on the tip of one of the bits of tinder.

It feels like I just created flame itself. "Yes," I murmur.

"Get it, did you?" Jackson asks.

"Of course," I say.

"Of course," he answers. "Because you're the type that does what she sets out to do."

"Yeah," I say. "I guess I am."

"I know you are," he says. "How's the smoke?"

I watch it, spiraling up through the flue—my word of the day. "I think it's going to be alright, though I guess we won't know until the fire's a little bigger."

"That'll be nice," he says. "Now come have a look at these cupboards. I've got the first few up."

I do, and nearly cry. The swirl of the natural wood is gorgeous in the old house. And with the soft-colored paint I've got in mind. I stop on that thought. I should have painted first. I sigh, the sound aching with the realization.

"You don't like it?" he asks, his voice dropping low.

"No," I say. "They're gorgeous, but I should have painted first. Now it'll take longer."

He nods. "I'm sorry. I assumed you wanted this color."

We both look at the avocado walls and then we both kind of laugh.

"You got the paint?" he says. "Maybe we could do it today and I'll finish these tomorrow."

"I've got the color," I answer, "but I'm not sure about brushes and things. I grabbed a packet of rollers and stuff, but I'm not sure if it's all we'll need."

"We'll make it work," he says. "You do the detail stuff over here where I've hung the cupboards—at least if that packet has tape. And I'll do the big stuff on these walls. You've gone and taken out the final wall, so at least we don't have to worry about it."

We both drag in the paint and rollers. Jackson

mixes and pours it into the pan. I start to tape. We don't have much, but it'll do for the one room. Together we paint in tall lines up and down. I'm losing myself in the meditation of it when Jackson asks, "What trailer park?"

"Excuse me?" I ask.

"Where were you raised?"

"It's not there anymore," I answer, avoiding the question.

"How long ago?" he asks, reaching to the top of the ceiling, his back broad and tight against the flannel shirt.

I blow out a breath. "I don't know. A while."

"You don't know?" he asks.

"I left when I was sixteen."

"So about thirty years ago," he says.

"Hey!" I say.

He laughs. "Never was good at math."

"Closer to twenty years, actually," I say. "Well, just seventeen. Seems like forever."

"Where'd your accent go?" he asks.

"I've got an accent," I say.

"Mmhmmm," he replies, taking a peek at the fire. "Smoke looks good. Flue is open."

"I was young when I moved," I say. "My accent shifted."

"Then what?" he says. "College up there? Or work?"

"Work," I answer. "Grocery store, then moved my way up to Target."

"Nice," he says.

"I liked retail, and got a job at the mall. Made it into management eventually."

"And?" he asks.

"And that's the end. That's where I am now," I say.

"But it's not where you want to be," he says.

"Well, I mean, I like it," I answer.

"But this house? You could just sell it. All fixed up, Mama says you could probably bring in nearly half a million dollars with all the land. Or you could lease it out to farmers and make it work for you that way."

"Say that again," I reply.

"You could lease the acres of land. People will rent it and farm it."

"And I could still keep the house, the gardens, the buildings?"

"Sure," he says.

"That's brilliant."

"Want my mama to call you about it?"

I look at him and I know it's unfair, but when he talked about his mama, the only lady I could imagine was an overly plump lady in a housedress drinking a lemonade with her thin hair piled up on her head. A Mama a little like my own. I realize in a rush that image probably wasn't correct. "You mother's a real estate agent." I say. It's not a question.

"Best in town," he answers.

"Then, yes, I would like her to call me," I reply. "Why didn't you tell me?"

"Didn't want you to feel pressure," he answers. "And I figured you already had someone."

"I do, but I don't think he does stuff with leasing. And your mother does?"

"Yes," he says.

"So I could lease a big chunk of this land? And still have the house?" My mind is running a mile a minute. "That, plus the Kickstarter."

"The what?" Jackson asks.

"A Kickstarter I'm doing to earn money for the renovation. People will pay for services ahead of time and I'll use the money to make these repairs."

"That where my paycheck is coming from?" he asks. He's turned to the wall, those big shoulders the only thing looking at me, but I can hear the smile in his voice.

"That or Memaw's ring."

"Ah, now," he says. "Don't sell that."

He puts the roller down. "First coat. Let's give it a few minutes." He glances at his watch and for the first time I notice it's a smart watch. Smart watch, smart Mama. I may have made some assumptions.

"Time for some snacks," I say, going to my box. The fire is beautiful and roaring now, all the smoke moving precisely upward. "Or maybe some celebratory hot chocolate."

I take the mugs, pour in the mix, and fill them with water.

"And where was that microwave?" he asks, glancing around.

"Memaw's bedroom," I answer.

"Ah," he says.

I don't add that I have no idea if it works or not, just go to the old bedroom like I'm sure it will.

And it does.

When the hot cocoa is warm, I plunk down cross-legged in front of the fire, patting the spot beside me.

Jackson joins me, sipping his drink. "All we need now is a little snow," he says with a laugh, moving over to open one of the heavy curtains in the living room.

And then we see it—the snow that has climbed up the window panes. At least six inches, actually closer to eight. It's still coming down hard, like it never intends to stop.

"Gretchen, you've got to get home," he says, setting his mug down with a plunk on the windowsill. "Now. Actually, three hours ago, but definitely now."

"But the paint," I object. "We need another coat."

"I'll do it," he says. "Today if you want, but you've really got to go. This is getting dangerous."

"What about you?"

"I can walk home if I need to," he says. "You can't."

I stand beside him at the window, watching it fall. I really do need to go.

"Come on," he says. "I'll help you clear the snow off your car and make sure you get out of the drive okay."

As soon as we step outside, I realize I've waited too long. The top layer of snow is soft and light, but down at the bottom, it's heavy and icy. I slip down the final step and Jackson catches my arm, steadying me. His face is hard, worried.

"Gretchen, let me call my mama. You can stay

there tonight. This ain't nothing worth going through."

"I've got to work tomorrow," I say. "It's fine." Though I'm feeling less and less like it's fine. Beneath my feet it's easy to see that it's more like ten inches. Ten inches in just a few hours. Lower tree limbs are dragging the ground from the weight. Even the power lines are hanging heavy. The snow fairies have outdone themselves.

"If it's this bad in Swallowsville, your store won't even be open."

I bite my lip, knowing he's right.

Jackson and I are both slipping and sliding to my car. He reaches out to take my waist, steadying me yet again. I turn to him, and I don't know what my face looks like, what it's saying, but I look up into his eyes, those wide copper discs. "Gretchen," he says, his voice low, thick, serious. "I'm calling my mother."

Which is maybe the least romantic line ever spoken. And why am I thinking about romantic lines when I might be stuck here in Midvale, trapped in an unfinished house with only a box of granola bars and a few cheese crackers to keep me company?

But then I look at Jackson again. He hasn't let go of my waist. In fact, now both of his hands are on either side of it. And I realize that I'm still looking up at him, and he's still looking down at me. And the flakes are falling, gathering all around us like we're the only two people on earth. He reaches down to move a lock of hair out of my face, leaves his hand on my cheek, the distance between us narrowing, the snow falling light and cold, though my whole body is warm, hot.

And then three very loud things happen. All at once.

Well, not quite all at once.

The first sound is a crash, hitting the side of the house. Which creates the second sound—an avalanche of snow and ice that cascades from roof to power line. Sparks flare, and then everything— including all the light in the house—goes dark. Which gives us a moment to hear the final sound— part scream, part howl, part wail. Coming from the place of impact.

Jackson is running before I can process any of the sounds, much less put them together into a coherent series of events.

And then I'm skating and stumbling after him through the snow. In the dimming light, I can see smoke rising up from the place of the first sound— the crash. When I turn the corner, an ATV, still running, is flipped over, tracks leading from the woods near the back of Memaw's property. I'm still not quite putting the details together, but they're kind of lumping in my brain.

Jackson is bending over something—the source of the howl. I look up at the power lines. They're sinking low, but nothing is scraping the ground and nothing is still sparking. In the strange way of this strange scene, that's a good thing.

The screaming voice is swearing and praying at the same time as Jackson coos at him, back hunched over the body. I see two legs, one of them bent at an excruciating angle, and I see dark spots in the snow around him.

Even though my brain is having trouble connecting to itself, some part of it is communicating with my fingers. 911. The soft, calm voice on the other line.

"Hi! There's been an accident. ATV. It crashed near my memaw's—near my house."

The dispatcher asks if the person is conscious. I can barely hear her question through his screaming and answer 'yes.'

"We'll have a unit there as soon as we can. Give me your address, please."

I do.

"Please hurry," I say. "It looks very serious. There's blood, and—" I stop, suddenly feeling nauseous and a little dizzy.

"Ma'am."

"Yes," I say, trying to gather myself. "He's very hurt."

"Is anyone else injured or involved?" she asks. Then, "A unit is on its way, right now."

"I don't think so," I say. "No one I can see." I realize as the words come out that there could have been someone else, someone thrown, someone silent. But I don't say that. I guess we'll all know soon enough.

It's getting dark quickly. And the snow around the man is dark too. I look away.

"How long?" Jackson asks me.

I repeat his question into the phone.

The dispatcher pauses, not for long, just this beat that I feel. It's a beat that scares me. "As soon as possible, ma'am, but we've got several units out already. And the snow is very bad. I'm hoping a unit will be there within thirty minutes, but the time could vary."

I step away from the scene, from the place where the injured man can hear me, whisper. "I think he's dying."

"We are getting a unit there as quickly as possible. I've dispatched a firetruck too."

"Is there, like, a helicopter or something?" I ask. "Something faster." Because I know the nearest hospital is in town, which is a solid thirty minutes away on a non-snowy day.

"The ground unit would normally make that call," she says. "But with this weather, the helicopters can't fly anyway."

I whisper my own little curse/prayer into the phone.

"Thank you," I say, hanging up and then wondering if I was supposed to stay on the line.

With the snow and the coming darkness, the temperature is dropping quickly.

I go back to Jackson. The man has settled a bit, though now I can see he's not a man at all—just a teenage boy.

"How long?" Jackson repeats.

"They're not sure," I answer, "but she said the snow is bad and they've got several units out."

He mutters his own little prayer/curse, minus the prayer part.

"It seems tricky to move him," Jackson mutters—whether it's to me or to himself, I'm not sure. "But he's going to freeze to death out here." He looks up at me through the still-falling snow. "Gretchen, can you bring me one of those sheets of plywood? We'll roll him on and take him by your fire."

My fire. It seems like a whole lifetime ago that I lit it. So fun, so cozy. Now a boy will be bleeding to death in front of it.

No, I tell myself, going inside—fighting through the snow, which is now easily a foot deep, more than I ever remember seeing in my life—to get the plywood. There's a six foot piece leaning against the one of the walls, and I drag it through the door, then over the snow like a sled.

"That'll do," Jackson says. "Can you help me, Gretchen?"

I can literally smell the blood, see the steam from where it is fresh. But I close my eyes and nod. Of course I can help him. "What if his back is broken?" I ask. I know you're not usually supposed to move people who are this hurt.

"He's too cold," Jackson says. "And he's probably suffering from shock. And it'll take too long for the ambulance to get here. We'll have more luck inside no matter what."

Then, like he's been doing this sort of thing every day of his life, Jackson tilts the boy's body to the side, instructing me to shimmy the plywood underneath.

He settles the boy back down and we drag him over the snow to the back door. Which is too small to go through.

"I'll get the sliding glass," I say. "Take him there."

Hurrying into the house and stumbling over the paint and brushes, the furniture that isn't mine, I find the sliding glass in the living room, unlock it, and tug. It doesn't budge. Clearly, it hasn't been used for a long time. "Come on," I mutter, pulling with all my weight against the handle. It finally gives, scraping along the track.

Jackson is there with the makeshift sled, and I try not to look at the trail of blood the boy has left.

"In we go," he says gently to the boy, but I can't help but notice that the boy does not respond.

As he drags the boy to the fire on the makeshift cot, I put more wood on, trying to pump it up from the embers it has become.

"Thanks, Gretchen," Jackson says, and a bit of a light flickers inside me. "How long has it been?" he asks, looking out the window.

"I don't know." Twelve seconds or a whole life-time. They feel the same right now. Jackson looks outside. It's getting dark now, the snow still coming down hard, which brings the minute blessing of lightening the sky. "I guess at least twenty minutes."

"I'm going to look for some supplies." He heads toward Memaw's bathroom.

I check my phone. I called twenty-two minutes ago. But outside everything is completely still. No sirens, not the smallest hint of an approaching vehicle. I listen for the boy, for his breathing. It's there, along with a thin whimper. And somehow in the silence of a house with no power, I can even hear him shivering. Not good.

I take an old blanket from one of Memaw's old couches and wrap it around him. Then I click my phone, 911. It's the same voice. She sounds tired. "Is this an emergency?" she asks with thin patience.

"I called twenty minutes ago," I say. "About the boy in the ATV accident." I give her the address.

She sighs. "I'm sorry, ma'am. Roads are closed or blocked with snow. Several of our units are trapped. We're working with the city snow plows as well as local volunteers to get them out."

"How long?" Jackson asks, coming back into the room with a bag as well as a couple of candles, which he hands silently to me.

As though the dispatcher has heard him, she continues, "It will be several hours."

The words cut off my breath. "Are you sure?" I

ask, cradling the phone against my shoulder and lighting the candles as Jackson leans over the boy.

"We're doing our best, but ma'am, there are *several* serious calls right now. And the roads are impassable."

Jackson takes the phone from me, speaking quickly, medically.

I'm close enough that I can hear her answers. "We're calling outside agencies for help right now. Yours is one of several serious calls. We're trying to make it to them all."

And now it's Jackson's turn to sigh. "Thank you," he murmurs, clicking off the phone and handing it back to me without glancing in my direction.

I look at him, at the backboard, at the bandage. "You're a paramedic," I say, thinking of Becca's boyfriend, Lance.

He shakes his head, ignoring me.

"A doctor?"

Another shake.

"Then what?"

Almost a smile as he lays a thick blanket over the torso of the boy. "A nurse," he answers. "ER."

Using a flashlight he's found, he begins to assess the boy from top to bottom.

"Gretchen, get some hydrogen peroxide for his

head. There's some in that bag from your memaw's bathroom. These cuts aren't great, but they're not the worst."

They look pretty bad to me. His head is crusted with blood, although even in the thought I realize that if they're getting crusty, that maybe is good.

"What *is* the worst?" I whisper, obediently digging for the hydrogen peroxide with the light from my phone's flashlight.

Jackson takes out the scissors Memaw probably used for sewing, and proceeds to cut the pants off the boy, all the way to his hip. "This is," he says.

I glance down at the boy's leg and quickly glance back up. The leg is not lined up like it should be.

"Hurts," the boy whispers.

"I imagine," Jackson says, covering most of his body with the blanket. "Looks like you've broken a bone."

I notice Jackson doesn't say which one. And I'm no expert, but from the looks of things, I'd guess it's his femur. And you don't have to be an expert to know that that's not good.

I turn my attention back to the boy's face, dabbing at the blood as gently as I can. Underneath the blood, the boy is ghost white and still shaking.

Taking an edge of the blanket, I tuck it up around his head, trying to keep him warm.

The boy responds with a moan, though it seems to have more to do with his leg than his face.

"You gonna set the bone?" the boy asks Jackson.

"Not my area of expertise," Jackson says, looking out of the windows at the snow that's still billowing down. "But I'm thinking it's going to be a spell before they can get a crew here. You up for a game of cards?"

And the kid, he kind of smiles. "Maybe a little Jack Daniels."

"I thought about it," Jackson says. "Might take the edge off, but I'm worried about keeping you hydrated. How about a little water instead? Gretchen, can you get him some?"

I hop up like the best nurse's assistant in the world, and hurry into the kitchen for a water bottle. When I walk back in, I hear the kid asking, "That your girlfriend?"

Jackson is piling pillows under and around his leg in a strange way. "Nah," he says. "I ain't that lucky."

"Here we go," I say, announcing my entry, as I hurry to the boy.

"What's your name?" Jackson asks the boy, shimmying a pillow close to the broken leg.

The boy curses, and I give Jackson a what-are-you-doing look.

"Just trying to get that leg secure, maybe create a little traction so it's lined up as best as we can get it."

I dig through Memaw's first aid bag and am surprised to find a couple of straws that have probably been around since the invention of plastic, but will do the trick. Holding a straw to the boy's lips, he takes a shivering sip of water.

"And what was your name?" I ask again. "I didn't catch it."

"Andy," he answers. Then, "You don't live here."

"This was my memaw's house," I answer.

"She died," he asks. Or maybe he states; it's unclear.

"A few months ago," I answer.

"Little crazy, wasn't she?"

I shrug. "Wouldn't surprise me, but I didn't really know her."

"Why'd she leave you this house then?" he asks, sounding more like a boy than the teenager he is.

"I guess because she was a little crazy," I say.

"You best be thanking that crazy lady," Jackson says to the boy. "'Cause she kept her bathroom stocked with a bunch of supplies. Without that, you'd be hurting a lot more."

I'm honestly wondering why he's not hurting more, why he's not screaming or crying. I'll have to ask Jackson later. Maybe something to do with adrenaline.

Before I can get Andy another sip of water, he's fallen asleep. Jackson is like a mother hen. Clucking around and fluffing pillows, or shoving them tight against him, checking his temperature with his hand, looking at the crooked thigh with the big bruises forming around the break.

"It's bleeding inside," he says, almost to himself.

"Is that normal?" I ask. "Or very bad?" I whisper the last part, even though the boy is still asleep.

"Normal, yes," Jackson says. "But also still bad. He's going to need surgery on that leg."

"Poor kid," I say, looking at his face. Then, thinking of TV shows I've seen. "Is it bad that he's sleeping? Aren't you supposed to keep them awake when they're in shock?"

"If it's a wakeful time. Right now, it's night. And I don't think it'll help to slap that kid awake every ten seconds. I'll wake him occasionally."

I look outside a little surprised to see how late it

looks. The moon is out now, just a few small flakes still falling. "It's finally slowed down," I say.

He nods.

I glance at my phone only to realize that it's dead. "How late is it?" I ask.

"Probably only about 7:30. Feels later though."

"My phone's dead," I say. "How is yours?"

"I put it on battery saver to try to keep it through the night. If I get desperate, I can go out and run my car to charge it.

"My gas is pretty low too," I say with a sigh.

"Came prepared for a big storm, did you?"

"It wasn't supposed to hit till tomorrow. Besides, I didn't believe them," I say, my voice pitching up in a way that makes Andy groan in his sleep.

Jackson bends over him. "I'm really not qualified for this type of thing," he says with a sigh. "I have no real equipment, nothing to be of help at all."

"Uh, incorrect," I say. "You're calm. You know what to do. I might have just run around in circles screaming."

"You wouldn't have. You did exactly the right thing and called 911."

"I almost barfed first," I say with a laugh, trying to let a little of the stress go.

"I *am* pretty good at not barfing," he says with a

subconscious glance at Andy's leg. "But expertise is still not much good without equipment."

"Untrue," I say. "He looks like a lamb."

Jackson takes that as his cue to jostle Andy's shoulder until he groans and wakes just a bit. "You doing okay?" he asks, looking into the pupils.

"Yeah, man." Then a groan, then back to sleep.

"He won't sleep all night," Jackson says. "Adrenaline will wear off and then he'll be in some serious pain. Speaking of, you ought to head to bed. Even if it's a little early."

"I am not sleeping in my dead memaw's bed," I say.

"We used her peroxide," he counters.

"That's different," I say.

"I'm sure there are other beds in this house."

"Who even knows who slept in those?" I answer. "Besides, you're not sleeping."

"All the more reason for you to get a little. If I get too tired, someone needs to watch over this kid."

"So we take shifts," I say.

"Yes," he answers. "You first. Take the couch if you want."

It's as good as anything. There's an old quilt draped over it, probably filled with dust and old spiderwebs, but still warm. Which is nice because, fire or no, the house is getting colder.

"Hope the pipes are okay," I murmur.

"Go turn the faucets on just a bit so they can drip," he says. "That'll help."

I nod, getting up and taking a candle so I can see my way through the house. "Why didn't you tell me you were a nurse?" I ask from the kitchen.

"You never asked," he said. "And it didn't seem relevant to the job."

"Well, Andy sure showed you," I say.

"He sure did."

In the kitchen, I notice that my stomach is growling. We never ate.

I gather up a few granola bars and a package of cheese crackers. Then stir the now cold mugs of cocoa, take it all in on a platter with a bar of nice dark chocolate.

"Dinner is served," I say, setting it down and putting the mugs as close as I dare to the fire.

"Oooh, fancy," he answers, picking up a cracker. "And you must be a good cook because I didn't realize I was hungry until this moment."

I laugh. "One day I'll really do a little cooking for you, and then you'll see what hunger is. And satisfaction."

He lifts his eyebrows, and I realize what I said, then hurry out of the room to turn more faucets on to drip.

Jackson's phone rings just as I come back in.

"Baby, where are you?" I can hear the female voice through the phone, and a tiny prick of jealousy stabs into my gut. The woman sounds a little panicked.

"Hi, Mama," he says. "I'm a little stuck at that house I was working on."

The prick of jealousy loosens up.

"I've got Paul coming in the morning," Jackson's mother says. "He'll clear you a path." She's still loud. A little deaf maybe, or maybe just a little loud.

"Any chance he can come before morning?" Jackson asks, glancing quickly at his battery. "Some kid got in an ATV accident down by the house. He's pretty tore up."

"How tore up?"

"Broke a femur."

"Dear heavens."

"I'll call Paul. You alone out there?"

Jackson glances at me. "Nah, the owner is here. Gretchen."

"I remember her name," his mother says. And

maybe there's a universal thing about moms with thirty-something sons.

"Let me know if he's coming," Jackson says in response, keeping his voice low, like he's trying to get his mom to do the same.

She doesn't. "Keep that girl warm," she says in good-bye. There's definitely a universal thing about moms with thirty-something sons. Also, I decide she's not deaf, just loud. I like her anyway.

"Love you Mama."

And the phone clicks off.

"Paul?" I ask.

"You heard the call?" he says.

"Mostly the beginning when she was worried and talking loud," I say, telling a bit of a half lie.

Jackson laughs. "She always talks loud. She's a big kind of lady."

"And who's Paul?" I say, reminding him.

"Her boyfriend," he says.

I nod. "And your dad?"

"Passed on," he answers and that's all.

"You like the boyfriend?" I ask.

"I do," he answers.

"Hmmm," I say. "Sounds boring."

"Paul's a good guy," he says. "Good for Mama. But

I don't want another dad. He seems to understand that."

"Well, you are in your thirties," I say. "None of us need another dad."

"Well, some could use a new one," he says. "That's one thing I've learned from the ER."

I don't dare to respond to that one. I don't have to because he keeps talking. "My dad had a heart attack a few years ago. Couple years after we lost Essie, my sister. Wasn't the easiest time."

"I'm so sorry," I say.

"Me too," he says. "But it's what inspired my current profession. The day job," he says with a laugh. "Not the side hustle, though I guess he inspired that too by teaching me how to fix stuff."

The boy—Andy—groans. Jackson shuffles over to him, feeling his forehead. When he's satisfied that the kid's not tossing with fever, he turns back to me. "Now you go sleep."

I lie down obediently, tucking the afghan around me, though it seems impossible to sleep with an injured boy and a cold room and a gorgeous nurse/handyman nearby. *Handy-man,* I hear in my head. Thanks a lot, Macie.

I curl toward the couch, hoping to warm up. And only realize I've fallen asleep a few hours later when

I hear the boy wake with the most blood-curdling scream I've ever heard. Like, wonder-if-Jackson-is-really-a-serial-killer scream. But Jackson has just hopped up from his chair, looking bleary-eyed. The fire is mostly ember.

Somehow the kid has managed to turn to his side in his sleep, which hurt his leg.

"Back you go," Jackson says softly, and the boy is crying.

I get up, dig through Memaw's bag and find a bottle of old Ibuprofen. "Will this help?" I ask.

From the look on Jackson's face I see a 'no,' which is why I'm surprised when he takes the water bottle and a couple pills. "Drink up," he says to Andy.

The boy's tears shift down to a whimper and he sips, then takes the pills.

"Hand me a square of chocolate, will you, Gretchen?"

He gives the chocolate to Andy. "That'll help it settle better in your stomach."

"I hurt everywhere," Andy says, though he's stopped crying.

"I bet you do," Jackson replies, shoving pillows back into place, trying to keep the leg from moving. "Now try not to move if you manage to fall back to sleep."

Andy settles, moving his arms to get comfortable.

"Will the medicine help?" I whisper when it seems he's asleep.

"Not likely," Jackson whispers back, "but sometimes it helps people just to think that something is helping."

I shiver and Jackson tucks the blanket over my shoulders. "A little chocolate?" he asks.

I smile. "Just what the doctor ordered."

"Nurse," he corrects with his own smile, breaking part of the chocolate bar off and handing it to me. "You've been a great help," he says.

"I've been a lot of nothing," I reply, getting up to put more wood on the fire.

"Well, what was that then?" he asks, motioning to the fire and then patting the spot beside him on the couch.

"You got the wood, brought the wood in," I reply.

"And you started that fire."

"I got us stuck here," I say.

"Nah, that was Andy," he replies. "And truth be told, I'm glad we were here when he crashed. Heaven only knows what would have happened to him if he'd been stuck in the snow all night."

I look into Jackson's eyes when he says it. The

coppers are bronze in the darkness. "What would have happened?"

"It's awfully cold," Jackson says. "And he would have had to crawl to shelter. I don't know. As it is, he's gonna be fine, but out there."

Jackson's face has gotten closer to mine as we've whispered, trying not to disturb Andy in his sleep.

"I'm glad we were here," I say, leaning in even closer.

"I'm glad we *are* here," Jackson responds and his voice has pitched down a step, husky and warm, just like the room suddenly is, our faces close, moving closer.

When suddenly Andy's eyes flash open. "My phone," he says. "Is it still in my pocket?"

Jackson and I spring apart, and I wrap myself up tight in the blanket as Jackson moves down next to Andy. "Probably dead if it is," Jackson replies. "It's nearly midnight."

The boy is wiggling and digging, unaware that most of his pants have been cut off.

"Stay still," Jackson says.

"Where is it?" Andy repeats, a little desperately.

"Maybe in the snow," Jackson says. "We'll look in the morning."

The boy is starting to sniffle again. "My mom," he says.

Jackson nods, a look passing over his face like he should have thought of this before. "She doesn't know where you are?" he asks.

"I told her I was going out."

"Give me her number," Jackson says.

"I don't know it," he answers.

Jackson mutters a curse. "Well, give me her name and I'll have my own mama get a hold of her."

"Marcie Patterson," the boy says.

"Where's she work?" Jackson asks.

"Down at the high school."

"Good," Jackson says. "That number'll be easy enough to find if Mama don't already know her."

"Who's your mama?" the boy asks.

"Charlene Wilson."

"Same lady from the real estate signs?"

"The one and only."

"My mama don't like her," the boy says.

"Well, she will tonight," Jackson answers.

He's not wrong. Two phone calls later and both the mothers are best friends.

Jackson also gets the update on Paul, who should be here in an hour, two at the most. He's working his way along the road, still several miles away, but making progress with his truck and a little plow he hooks up to it.

"Well, kid, you'll be on your way to the hospital soon."

But Andy has already fallen back into a groaning sort of sleep.

"The sooner the better," Jackson says, sitting beside me again, though not quite as close as he was, not quite as close as I realize I wish he was.

"Try to get some sleep, Gretchen," he says.

"Maybe it's your turn," I answer.

"I can't sleep."

"That's what I thought," I say. "Give it a shot." I hand him a pillow, tuck it under his head. "See, nice, isn't it?"

He smiles, leaning his head on it and looking into my face. I want to reach out and touch his cheek, but he's closing his eyes, so I just watch him. The sharp cheekbones, broad forehead, auburn hair, the stubble of a beard filling in as the night progresses. It's a face I could get used to watching at night.

I lean my own head against the couch, shifting just a little closer to the warmth of his body. My eyes droop, so tired as the night wears on. The boy moans and I remember this is my shift. I'm supposed to be staying awake. I close my eyes. Just for a second. Just for one little second.

I wake to the sound of the back door. Jackson is carrying wood in and stirring the fire, which has nearly died. The candles have burned low and the room is freezing. He's piled more blankets on Andy, whose eyelids flutter.

He moans and shifts. "Dude, I've got to pee so bad."

Jackson looks at me. "Gretchen, you want to bring me a cup. And then step out for a second."

If I was Andy, I'd start to cry again. But men are different about this stuff. One cup and a few minutes later, Andy is closing his eyes, drifting off in that moaning, fidgeting way.

Jackson is looking outside into the darkness, the fire starting to crackle.

"I'm sorry," I say, "for falling asleep."

"That's okay," he answers. "It's hard to stay awake."

Andy is groaning and turning more now, trying to shift side to side against the pillow barricades that Jackson has built. "Blankets are heavy," he grunts. "They hurt."

Jackson removes one.

"I'm really sorry," I whisper, wishing Jackson

would come back and sit by me. Instead he's messing with the fire, the fire I should have been tending when I had my shift. My shift that I spent gazing into Jackson's face and then falling asleep.

"It's not a problem," he says. But in a way that feels like he thinks that now he's got to do it all.

"Should I give him another pill?" I ask.

"If he wants it," Jackson says.

But the boy is asleep, or at least not awake. I sit beside Andy on the floor. Jackson takes a swig of the cold cocoa and pops a few crackers in his mouth. "It's gonna feel good to get home, ain't it?" He's looking outside to the dark patch that is the long drive. "Just wish Paul would hurry. It's been forever."

I get up and stand beside him at the window.

"You really better sleep," Jackson says. "You've got that drive home in the morning."

"You think the roads will be okay?" I ask, hoping for…well, when I'm honest, hoping for maybe an invitation to sleep it off at his house. An invitation that is as ridiculous as it sounds when I've got my very own house right here, albeit without power.

"If the roads are shut down, I'll call Mama and you can stay there."

"Thank you," I say. "Are you mad I fell asleep?"

He looks over at me, his eyes tired, wrinkled, and

starting to puff a bit. "Nah, Gretchen. I'm just annoyed that I let myself fall asleep."

"You're exhausted," I say.

He smiles and if he was my brother he'd give me a hug. But I don't want a brotherly hug. Somehow I want to take us back to that place on the couch, faces close, noses close, mouths close. But everything feels careful and spaced now.

"Get some sleep."

It's not a question, not really a suggestion. I walk to the couch, find the afghan, curl up and snuggle in. But this time, for some reason, with all the permission in the world to sleep, I find that I can't. I roll over a few turns, pull the blanket over my cold face, try the deep breathing from my yoga class. But now my joints hurt and my mind is buzzing. When I peek through the blanket at Jackson, he's sitting next to Andy on the floor, with an exhausted stare, his head propped on his fist, and bobbing down every few seconds.

I take the blanket off, walk over to him, and drape it over his shoulders, then sit beside him, staring out the window. Gray dawn lines are stretching over the distant horizon and outside it's perfectly still. No sound of approaching sirens, no sound of approaching plows.

"I'll see if I can scrounge us up some breakfast," I say. "Maybe Memaw has something in the cellar or somewhere, something that isn't expired."

And she does.

It's my first foray into the cellar. I've been afraid to go down. But, even though I have to move the wood barricade out of the way, and even though the stairs are rickety and two are missing, I make it. I find rows of dusty shelves with several cans of peaches that are just short of expiring. Plus a couple bags of lemon tea shoved into the back, and a few cans of milk.

Back in the unfinished kitchen, I pop the milk open, drizzling it over the peaches. Then rinse the hot chocolate mugs, add water, and put the tea bags in. I'll do my best to heat them, but hopefully we can drag some energy out of those things no matter what.

Once again, I load it all onto the tray and bring it into the living room.

"You are an artist," Jackson says.

"Country living," I reply.

"It's the best," he answers, digging into his peaches and 'cream.'

"Well, it's something," I say, looking around.

"People are good in the country. Like family," he says.

I just shrug. The sun is beginning to brighten the room, dim light filtering through the windows, catching the pictures along the walls—pictures of Memaw and my dad and a bunch of other people I don't know. "I guess then the question is whether or not you want people to be like your family." An early morning sun ray settles on a portrait of Memaw holding a cherubic baby who is dressed in white, ready for a baptism or something. So far off from anything I ever knew of my family that it's hard to even put it together.

"Oh, come on, Gretchen," Jackson chides. "Surely you don't hate it here."

"Never said I did," I respond.

But Jackson doesn't let it drop. "Look at Mama and Andy's mom. Like sisters now."

"Only because of a tragedy," I reply.

"Exactly. In places like this, people pull together."

"Or apart," I say, noticing there are no more pictures of Daddy after about age twelve.

"Ah now, that's true anywhere," he says.

"Is it?" I ask. "Seems like it's truer in a place where everyone knows everyone else's business. After all, it's like *you* said—look at your mama and

Andy's mom. They didn't even like each other. Do you even know why?"

And if I know anything, I know that you don't go criticizing a country boy's mama. But it's been a long night and my nerves are worn thin and—I don't know—it just comes out.

"Well," Jackson says, finishing off his tea. "If I don't know why, doesn't seem like people know *everybody's* business, now does it?"

"Andy knows Memaw's," I say, looking at the boy sleeping at our feet. In the light, he looks much rougher than in the dark. You can see the cuts all over his face, the splotches of dried blood I missed, the bruising, and that leg, shifted just slightly to where it shouldn't be, swollen and purpling. "He knows more than I do about my own grandma."

"And whose fault is that?" Jackson asks, his own nerves worn thin, his own face tight at the daytime sight of Andy. He bends over him, reaching for the bottle of hydrogen peroxide, though it's hardly going to do much good now that everything has scabbed.

"You think it's *my fault*?" I say, and Andy shifts a little on the floor. "A little girl living in a trailer out in the hills?"

"Gretchen, calm down," he says, dabbing peroxide along wounds in Andy's hair that I missed.

I don't calm down. "Or maybe you think it's my fault now that I'm older. Now that I'm a big city girl sending those big city checks to a Memaw who managed to ask for cash almost every month, but never once invited me down to meet her."

"Seems like it paid off," Jackson says, his voice sharp. "Pun intended."

"If you're going to ask me to apologize for getting this house, I won't," I say, my accent dripping, then pouring through. "I'm not saying I *deserved* it, 'cause I sure didn't. But I am saying that it's a poor consolation prize for a life with no daddy 'cause he shot himself or drank himself to death. And I don't even know 'cause my mama wouldn't tell me. You know what I saw of him when he died?" I say, my voice rising higher than I realize it has. "His boot. His dirty, muddy boot."

And then somehow I'm crying, and somehow Jackson has his arms around me, his chin tucked over my head. "Shhh, Gretchen, it's okay. Shhhh."

And I'm not sure if he's shushing me because of Andy or something deeper, but I don't stop talking. I can't. "And then Mama practically ate herself to death. Not practically. She did. I was the one that took her limp body to the hospital. But she was gone by the time we got there. Gone. Her sugar crashed and unrecoverable. I didn't even graduate. Just stopped going to school. A few months later, after all the dust had settled, I gathered up every bit of cash and coin I could find in the trailer and made my way to Swallowsville—the closest city, that was my one requirement."

"Gretchen, it's okay," Jackson says again.

But it's not okay. "I started applying at jobs, lived out of my car, raked my way through every rack at the Goodwill. I bought a gym membership because I figured out that I could take a shower at the gym and that was cheaper than rent. Figured out that I could appear like I was better off than I was. Figured out how to put things together real pretty. Figured out how to talk better than I'd learned. And it worked. People helped me up there. My first boss told me how to get my GED. My second boss let me take over the clothing department. That was a heck of a lot better than some judgy old lady bringing a casserole after Daddy died, a heck of a lot better than people looking the other way to spare me my dignity after Mama died. Up there, people didn't have to spare me my dignity, because I HAD dignity. They gonna bake that into a pie?"

I pull away from Jackson. "I realized I was kinda good at things like color and style. I started my own business, and I did well with it. I moved up to management, and I did well with it. And then I got this house, and I plan to do well with it too. You gonna try to stop me or help me?"

Andy is awake now, not even moving, just staring.

"Gretchen," Jackson says.

"I swore I'd never come back. And I never would have if this house hadn't popped up. And with it a chance to fulfill a little dream."

"A dream to fix it and make a bunch of money?" Jackson asks.

"Well, yes, actually. And what's wrong with that? Do I have to be poor and still living in a trailer park somewhere to keep my place in this city?"

"No, you don't," Jackson says. "But maybe don't come back to the country because the only good reason is that you can make money off of it."

I pause before biting back, gather as much venom as I have, prepare to sink my fangs in, drive my argument—whatever that may be—home. But in the silence of that pause, we hear a little noise. The sound of an engine, and scraping. Like a miniature avalanche coming up the drive.

"Paul," Jackson says, rushing to the window. "I

gotta dig my car out, so we can get Andy to the hospital."

And then I'm there with a wide-eyed kid, who's surely convinced I'm every bit as crazy as Memaw, and then some.

"How much you hear?"

"Some," he answers.

"Working out a blackmail deal for later?" I say, feeling his forehead like Jackson did the night before. Thinking of that, and how tired Jackson must be, gives me a pang. I push it away.

"Not till you get rich off this house," he says.

I laugh. "Smart kid."

"You need a guy to work for you?" he says. "Give me a call."

My laugh settles into a smile. "Well, I might when it finally gets up and running. If I ever get this place up and running."

"You will," Andy says.

"Well, IF I do, I'll need servers and hosts and landscapers and who knows who else." I plunk onto the couch, all the fire burned out of me, just like it had in the hearth. "You warm enough?" I ask.

"Yeah," he says.

"How's the pain?"

"It's bad," he says.

"You're pretty brave about it."

"Country boy," he answers, and gives me a pointed look.

"Yeah, well, use that talent for something besides —" I pause, not sure how to finish the sentence. *Getting drunk or getting shot* seems a little too tactless under the circumstances. Even for the raging, country *me* who just popped out. "For something worthwhile."

"You ought to give my man Jackson a shot," Andy says, glancing through the kitchen to the back door.

We can both hear Jackson shoveling the snow.

"A shot at what?" I ask.

"He's a good dude, saved my life."

"He did," I say. "You would have frozen to death out there."

"I know," Andy says. "And you helped save me too. Thank you."

"You're welcome."

"Now don't be crazy, like your memaw. And give my boy Jackson a shot."

"Not sure your boy wants a shot," I say. "Especially after I lost my mind just now."

"Everybody loses their mind sometimes," Andy says. "I thought it was pretty mild, to be honest."

I laugh.

"And I been watching Jackson. Pretty sure he wants a shot," Andy says with all the wisdom and insider knowledge of a teenage boy.

At that moment, the power flickers on.

"See, even our holy Lord thinks you should," Andy says. "That's a sign."

"I'll consider this potential evidence," I say solemnly.

"Do," he answers with a wink.

And then the sirens.

"Halleluiah," Jackson says, coming in, stomping the snow off his boots, dusting it off his coat. He looks beautiful and rough and strong. And he doesn't even know it. "I thought I was going to have to drag this kid into the back of my truck."

A man comes in behind him—Paul I assume. "I'm gonna go out and widen the path," he says to Jackson, and then is gone again.

I slink around, moving pillows, looking down, trying to avoid Jackson's face. I completely lost it—went full-on crazy. But before I can apologize, the ambulance arrives in a blaze of glory. Which, to be honest, seems a little unnecessary considering they're the only vehicle on the road, much less Memaw's driveway, and it's 6:30 in the morning.

We both rush to meet them.

The driver hops out, as spry as a child. The passenger, an older man, moves more slowly.

"Hey, Jackson," the passenger says. "What are you doing here?"

"It's a long story," Jackson answers. "Our guy's in the house. He's been a trooper."

"How's his head?"

"Cut up, but fine," Jackson answers, walking them through the kitchen. "Femur's broken though."

The old medic lets out an impressive swear. And then we come to Andy, all walled in with pillows and blankets.

Both medics laugh.

"You're a lucky kid," the old guy says.

"I know, sir," Andy says.

They lay the backboard down as Jackson and I throw pillows out of the way. The medics roll Andy onto it so quickly I barely see it happen. In a few more seconds they've lifted him onto the cot, and he's out of the house.

"A wheelchair accessible ramp," Jackson says as we watch them load Andy up into the ambulance. Andy gives a thumbs-up as they shut the back ambulance doors.

"What?" I say, watching the ambulance.

"A wheelchair ramp," he repeats. "You'll want one

of those for your business. At some entrance in the house."

I nod, barely able to process what he's saying. "I'm really sorry about how I behaved," I blurt out.

"Don't worry about it," Jackson says, waving it away and picking up the shovel he was using to dig out his car. It's just a regular shovel; Memaw must not have had a snow one. I can hear Paul down the driveway, his little truck chugging away as it shovels the snow. "Everybody has a little country girl rage sometimes. Especially after a night like that."

"It wasn't 'country girl rage,'" I say, taking out my gloves and beginning to dust off my own car. "Or even 'back hills rage,' just bad manners."

"Well, everyone's allowed a few bad manners here and there," he answers. He opens his car door, or tries to. It takes a couple of jerks to get it to budge. "Especially if it was the type of hill you was raised on, so to speak." He lets his accent really take hold, emphasizes it, I realize.

I want to laugh, but still feel too embarrassed. "Maybe it was," I say, taking the shovel while he digs around inside his car for an ice scraper. "But that's no excuse now. It's been a lot of years."

"Home comes back to us," he says, scraping while I try to move snow off my windows without scratching the glass. "The good and the bad." He comes over to me and starts to help—handing me the scraper and taking the shovel, digging around the tires, then making a little path to the driveway that Paul has cleared.

"Or maybe just the bad," I say to myself. He looks up, and for a minute I think he might come in for a hug.

I step back, jerking at my own door. I've come a long way from those years, but the truth is they still hurt, hurt more than he can possibly understand.

"If you get tired, you need to pull over," Jackson says.

As he says it we both realize there won't be a place to pull over. Just a wall of snow on the shoulder of the road.

"Maybe you ought to go to Mama's."

"That's okay," I say. "I'll get home just fine." I still can't get my door open though, so the words don't seem super empowered.

"May I?" he asks.

I step to the side.

He jerks it open on the second try.

"Impressive," I say. "You go home and get some sleep too."

He doesn't answer me and I glance at him sharply. "You going home?"

"For a minute," he says. "Gotta change. My shift starts at seven."

"You're kidding," I say. "Surely you can call in."

"If it's slow, I'll beg off. Otherwise…" He shrugs. "You know they're going to be short staffed. And I'll probably get a chance to see Andy before he heads up for surgery."

I nod, and he nods. And then he gets in his truck, and drives away.

I watch the lights get smaller, and realize that this is how you lose a guy you didn't want because you thought he was jobless and too country. He just… drives off. But only after you realize he has a lot more education than you, not to mention useful, lifesaving, real-life skills. Only after you realize that if anyone is country, it's you.

Even after all these years.

Getting into my car, I realize that I pegged Jackson wrong from the start. And I held him to that for all these weeks we've known each other, missing the hints, the signs that he wasn't just an underemployed, fix-it guy after all. What a very country thing for me to do.

I roll the irony around in my brain.

I'm tired enough that I forget to charge my phone until about ten minutes from home. When it finally turns on, I realize I won't be getting much sleep at all, because the texts from yesterday keep popping up, one after another. Exuberant Kickstarter updates. Panicked where-are-you texts. Calls. Messages.

I text the girls first. Work second.

And realize after that I've got no one else to call. No Mama. No Daddy. Not even a Memaw.

And then I start to cry.

CHAPTER 17

Macie and Becca baby me as best they can.

Which means they putter around my clean apartment trying to figure out what to do. No pie. No casserole. I'm glad. I think.

They make me a pot of coffee, which I don't dare drink because I need to sleep. And Macie grabs some quick Mexican for me. I'm grateful for it, all of it. And I don't need much, don't need anything except to know they care, which I do. The thought brings me more comfort than any of the things they're actually doing.

It also reminds me that I'm the one who's best at babying people—I'd know just the gifts that an exhausted person would need—a fuzzy blanket, chamomile tea, a little silence, and someone to send a quick email to my boss to sort things out for the next day or so. Jackson was right. The store is closed, but I'm wondering when my boss thinks it will open and what shifts she's expecting from me if it does.

I give the girls the basics of what happened and tell Becca to wake me in five hours.

"You sure?" she asks.

"Positive," I say. "You've got news and I want to hear all about the Kickstarter."

"Sweet dreams full of news," she says, like she's just about to pee her pants. "It went really well."

When she comes back that evening, she does indeed have a casserole, one that Lance made. It's a classic broccoli and chicken, and it's perfect.

"So…" Becca says in that wiggly-pee-your-pants kind of way she's had ever since I got back. "I've got a little surprise coming." She watches me eat (I'm starving!), then checks the clock on her phone. "The queen of YouTube and Kickstarters and business."

"Your sister," I say.

"Yup," she answers. "She's gonna walk us through the awesomeness that is…Well, you just have to see it."

I scoot over, moving my food. I'm not quite ready to stop eating, but she plops her laptop down on my table and opens it up. "I'm not gonna lie. It was a slow start. I didn't think we would hit it. That's why I didn't call you when you still had a charged phone. It just all felt like bad news. But then Sally…" Becca pauses and I glance at her and realize she's teared up just a bit. "Well, she bought something and then she posted it to her socials. And then…bam. She's a bam kind of person," Becca says.

I see where it happens during the campaign. As though we're watching Sally Mae post in real time—the spike in orders. Girl's nights, book clubs, even one wedding reception.

"We reached our Level One goal within that hour. That's when I first called you. And before I lost my mind with panic."

"And then?" I ask, popping a broccoli in my mouth, and scooping more onto my plate.

"We reached our second level within the next hour. Just like that. It was spreading and people were sharing. It was—" She tears up again.

"Incredible," I say, looking at the numbers and charts.

"Yes. And I wanted to get a hold of you, but your phone was going to voicemail. And I knew you'd gone down to the house, and the snow. Oh my gosh, it was terrifying."

"I'm so sorry. I didn't even think to check in and then my phone died. I should have gone out to charge it in my car."

"No," she says. "It's okay. I made Lance call around to his friends in different places—to make sure no Gretchens or Jane Does had been scraped up off the road. None had, and that made me feel better. But then the only person I could call with the good news was Macie."

Right on cue, Macie lets herself in. "I heard my name."

"I was complaining about having to call you with my Kickstarter news when I couldn't get a hold of Gretchen."

"Consolation prize," she says.

"I had to tell someone," Becca says. "So I gushed it all to Macie."

Macie nods. "I even squealed in delight and everything."

"She did," Becca says.

And I'm kind of giggling and stuffed and tired, but even now as I'm watching Becca's laptop, the numbers are climbing. "It's not stopping," I say.

"I think you're going to have the money to fix the house," Becca says. "You won't even have to haul off any more corpse refrigerators. You can hire people to do the rest of the tear out. And get back to your regular life."

I look down, focusing on my casserole.

"Tell handy-man to get a crew," Macie adds.

I push a piece of broccoli around on my plate. They both see it.

"What happened?" Becca says.

"Something very good, or very bad," Macie says.

"No," I say. "Neither. He was just there, helping me. And then that kid hit the house and broke his leg and he…helped."

"That sounds good," Macie says.

"So you spent the *night* in the house with him?" Becca says, staring at me.

"Well, technically," I say. "He was taking care of that kid—Andy. And I was tending the fire and trying to help Jackson."

"You were helping *him*?" Becca asks.

"He's an ER nurse."

Macie raises her eyebrows. "Plot twist. But not, like, a billionaire doctor or something? Not that kind of plot twist?"

"Well, no," I say. "But a nurse. He saved that kid—Andy would have frozen to death if Jackson hadn't been there."

"You wouldn't have let him freeze to death either," Becca says defensively.

"No, but I wouldn't have known what to do. The ambulance couldn't get there. And you should have seen the blood and his leg. I almost threw up."

"But you didn't," Becca says.

"And you spent the night with handy-man?" Macie says again, digging.

"Neither of us slept a lot," I grumble.

And then Macie giggles, and Becca does too. I look at them like they're nuts, until I realize what I said.

"No, not like that." I start laughing too. "We were trying to keep this kid from going into shock."

"Bet it was *so* cold," Macie crows.

"Oh, Jackson," Becca says in a dramatic, damsel-in-distress voice. "We'd better stay warm by lying together upon this couch."

"My memaw's couch, guys. Gross," I say.

But Becca's not done. In that same breathy, high voice, "Whatever would I do without the simmering heat from your manly body."

"Why yes," Macie says, pitching her voice low. "And I had to remove my shirt and tear it into shreds in order to save this young man, so now I'm utterly shirtless. Come to the warmth of my flesh, so we do not perish."

"You got me, guys," I say. "That is *exactly* how it went down."

"Knew it," Macie says. Then, because she just can't resist. "*Handy-man.*"

"Heaven help us, if you ever actually have a full conversation with him."

"Oh, I'm hoping to," Macie says.

Becca pops her eyebrow. "We should all have dinner together."

I look from one friend to the other, my smile kind of melting off my face. "Yeah, probably not. Even if he does finish the job for me."

"If…?" Becca says.

I look at the cooling casserole. "I said some rude things about living in the country. I was just tired. And it had been a stressful night. And…I don't know."

"What things?" Macie asks.

"Nothing too shocking," I say. "Just…stuff. But also, I was so convinced that he was country, and I kind of treated him that way—maybe like people used to treat me. With this bias. But then it turns out that he actually has more education and skills than I do. And there's something about it. Like, I wasn't even considering him because I thought he was too beneath me or something. But he's really above me."

On that note, Sally Mae arrives.

She's brought me a set of soft, warm pajamas and slippers to match. The perfect gift, like one I would have found.

"Every girl boss needs a good set of slippers," she says, sliding into the chair beside me.

Becca's sister is her counterpoint in just about every way. Sally's on the short side, curvy and soft in an almost matriarchal way. Ginger hair, freckles. Pink lips, sweet smile. Nothing sleek or hulking about her. But when she walks in the room, you feel it. There's something *power* about her. When she talks, you listen.

And she talks, and I listen.

She points to the graphs, to the orders, to the total money earned. She goes through fees and taxes and obligations. She pulls out a huge calendar and we go through it, charting when and how to get all the arrangements made. "You'll need to get the house fixed, but even before it's done, you've got to hire yourself a caterer, an accountant, and maybe a lawyer. It's not a game anymore, baby doll."

I nod stupidly.

"And that's a good thing," she continues. "Because

who wants to play games when there's money to be earned."

"Ah, that's my sister for you," Becca murmurs fondly.

"Don't get me wrong," Sally Mae says. "You're going to have fun. You're going to have a lot of fun. But you're going to work your tush off too."

"Thank you," I say. "I'm not sure I ever could have not messed this up without you."

"Oh, you could still mess it up, baby," she says with a smile. "But you call me when you need to and we'll try to keep that from happening."

"So, first?" I say. I'm having a hard time wrapping my brain around it all. It's just too big. "First, what? Give me a week's overview."

"The Kickstarter will go for several more weeks. That's good. It'll give you a second to breathe. Use this time to hop on your socials and blare it to the world."

"Okay." My "socials" are one slightly abandoned Facebook page and an Instagram I use to get makeup ideas.

"Also, get a real contract with your construction team."

Handy-man, I hear Macie's voice in my head. "It's just one guy right now."

She nods like I'm insane, but she's going to try to work with it. "Well, get a solid contract, with an end date. If he can't give you one that has the job finished within the next three months, find a new guy. Or, maybe a new *company.* Preferably a contractor who handles all aspects of house repair—plumbing, electric, permits, the whole thing."

I'm jotting things down as quickly as she says them. "I was tearing the kitchen out, and we were in the middle of painting when the power went out. Should we, I, finish that up?"

"If that's what you agreed to do, you can," she says. "But I would just call your current construction guy and see if he can do it. It might cost more, but it will save you time. And you're going to need a little of that." She gestures to the calendar.

"Okay," I say in a small voice.

"A little overwhelming, isn't it?" she asks.

I nod, looking down at my notes, at the word 'contractor,' which I've circled three times. I wonder if Jackson will actually be relieved to be released from the house.

"Take next weekend and go down there," Sally says, a little more gently. "Talk to your repairman. Have a written contract ready with what you want. I'll give you the name of my lawyer. Anyway, create an itemized list of jobs and prices. And if your repairman can't do it, move along. You want to get this business going by December so you don't miss the holidays completely. It's go time, darlin'."

Right. Go time. Which I'm normally 100% good at, but it's like my brain is talking southern-slow, and I'm struggling to hold everything in my hands.

"Take it a bite at a time," Becca says, giving Sally a pointed look.

"Yes," Sally agrees. "First bite: Meet with your contractor. Get a firm understanding of what he can do. And then make plans to hire out the rest."

"Just when I was getting my country sway on," I say, thinking of Jackson.

"You can find that again later," she says. "When you're hosting. Now it's time for a bit of New York City hustle." She gives me a hug. It's warm and slow. When she pulls me back, she looks into my eyes. "Congratulations, Gretchen. Becca says this is a dream come true for you."

"It is," I say. At least it was when it was all abstract and let's-fix-a-house-it'll-be-fun.

Sally winks. "One bite at a time. And call me."

"I will."

"For real," Becca says when she's gone. "Call her."

"Oh, I meant it," I say, looking at the calendar she's left. "I don't know how I couldn't."

"And when you have to cry, you can still call us," Becca says.

We all look at the computer, the Kickstarter numbers still rising, the names of the patrons floating across the screen. And then I do just that—cry, then laugh, then do a combo of both.

Becca and Macie surround me—a little circle of friends.

Nearly lost in the crush of Kickstarter memos and to-do notifications is the little reminder about my job interview. All the way in Louisville.

I'd almost forgotten about the whole thing—with a kid almost dying on my property and then the Kickstarter blowing up and all. Thank heavens for cell phones, or I might have missed it entirely. As it is, the interview is going to be crammed between a series of phone calls, furniture purchases, and interviews of my own to find the perfect caterer.

In fact, I'm glad I'm headed to Louisville because it gives me the opportunity to talk to a few of the potential caterers in person. Though truthfully, I am still hoping to find someone a little closer to home.

I button my blouse, and throw on a red jacket. Power suit, with a flair. My hair is up in a braided knot with a few strands framing my face. Subdued makeup with a pop of color for my lips. I lean toward the mirror. Do I look like more than a branch manager? Or do I look like a successful businesswoman, the kind of girl who could work in upper management, travelling around to different stores and getting them running as smoothly and profitably as possible?

I realize that I *do* look that way. But deep down inside, I'm not quite sure that I feel it.

I'm not really sure how interviews for top tier positions are supposed to go, but everyone smiles a lot, especially me. In fact, by the time I complete the first level with Jane Matthews, the woman who emailed me, my cheeks are already aching. My shoulders too, if I'm being honest.

It's at that point that level two begins. Meaning Jane brings in Mr. Perry Lambert, whom I gather is kind of a big deal. At least that's how it looks from the way she moves to the side, allowing him to sit before she does. And as opposed to Jane, who invited me almost immediately to use her first name, Mr. Lambert keeps it all business. So now, in addition to my aching cheeks, I'm starting to sweat.

Even so, things are going…well. We talk design, color, dishes, clothes, fashion, and employee disputes. They both seem pretty pleased with my answers. At least until they get to the bit about my education. Mr. Lambert stops, his finger resting on one line of the page. I have a pretty good idea of what that line says.

Jane jumps in. "Gretchen, Mr. Lambert and I noticed a bit of a gap in your education."

Mr. Lambert raises his eyebrows like that's the understatement of the century.

"We were wondering," Jane goes on, "if you would be open to completing online classes with the intention of gaining a business degree."

"A college degree?" I say.

"Yes," Mr. Lambert says. "In business."

I nod, tasting the word on my mouth. *Business degree.*

They must misinterpret my pause because Jane jumps in, "Of course, our company would pay for the courses."

"As long as you maintain a certain standard in the classes," Mr. Lambert quickly adds.

"Of course," I say, like I talk about getting a college degree every day. A college degree in business. "And that would be wonderful. I've always wanted to go to college, but life threw a couple of curve balls at me."

"Yes," Mr. Lambert says, looking to my file. And that's when I know that I'm not getting the job. His forehead is a whole series of wrinkles, pressed up hard against his scalp. "Could you, would you, care to elaborate a little on that. Your work history is great, your references impressive, but your schooling—well, it's a little out of the norm for us."

I clear my throat. "My mother died when I was in high school," I say, trying to keep it as simple as possible. "It, uh, threw me off a bit. Well, a lot. My Daddy, uh, father, had died years earlier, so after my mother passed, there was a lot of business to be done. School suddenly didn't seem that important." I clear my throat again. "At the time. When I was so young."

Mr. Lambert nods, still not looking into my face, but Jane leans back in her chair, smiling. "It's been delightful to chat with you," she says, gathering the stack of papers in front of them. "We'll look over all of this, and be in touch."

I don't ask when she expects that to be. I don't

ask any other questions at all. I know what it means to 'be in touch.'

And that's okay. Because I've got an old house to fix.

CHAPTER 19

*I*t's time to get things moving. And quickly. Finish painting, clear my tools out of the house. Move forward.

It's also time to talk to Jackson—see what his timeline is, suggest to him that maybe I should hire someone else to get it moving more quickly.

It's not a conversation I'm looking forward to.

But when I walk into the farmhouse, I'm shocked to see that the kitchen is completely done. Cupboards up, walls painted, sink installed. I run my fingers along the marble countertop I chose, little flecks of glitter popping out of the dark granite.

The curtains and blinds are down so the paint can dry. Paint I didn't have to do. And without the window coverings, the sun shines through in streaks of yellow that hit the walnut cupboards. The sink sparkles at me. The floors aren't refinished yet, but everything is swept and clean.

My own supplies are stacked neatly where the refrigerator will be when it comes later today—a couple of nearly empty paint cans, some brushes Jackson didn't use, and a drop cloth.

I remember him behind me, reaching up to paint the high parts, our bodies close together, the smell of him mixing with the smell of the paint.

I don't even hear the click of the door opening. Which means I don't know how long he's been standing there before he says, "Hey, Gretchen," and I jump ten thousand feet into the air.

"You scared me," I say, and it's not the thing I want to say.

"What do you think?" he asks.

"It's gorgeous," I respond. "I had no idea you'd be working on it so much this week."

"I wanted to get it done, so I can get out of your hair," he says. "You've got big things coming."

"Did you hear about the Kickstarter?" I ask.

"Kickstarter?" he says. "Nah, I just see it in you." He walks around. "The house is going to come together real pretty. Don't you think?"

"I do," I say, looking through the hole in the wall

to the place where we sat on the couch, watching over Andy, and apparently not falling in love like we were supposed to when we were trapped in a house during a snowstorm.

"I'll get to that wall this week," he says, misunderstanding my gaze at the hole.

"Sure," I say. "That sounds great. Jackson, it's really just...top notch."

Is that all I can say?

He smiles. "My daddy taught me to do good work."

I look at him. "I said some things last time that I regret. I was tired, and all my filters..."

"I already told you, Gretchen. No worries. This town is your home too. You use it how you see fit."

"I mean, I don't really want to *use* it," I say. "Like, not in the way people use things just to...you know, take advantage of them."

"This land wasn't good to you. Maybe now it can be," he says.

I blink, unsure of how to respond.

"I'll send you my bill in the mail," he says. "Do you have people to do the rest of the house? Floors and stuff. I've got some names..."

"My friend recommended a contractor she said

was good. His company does…well, I think they do pretty much everything."

"Perfect, then," he says.

I notice that he's wearing scrubs, off to work.

"Jackson," I start again. "I feel like I need to apologize."

"You already did," he interrupts, his back already to me. "Multiple times. You don't need to anymore."

"No," I say. "Really. Please, just hear me."

He turns back.

"I'm gonna level with you," I say. "When I met you, when I came here, I did think of it all as a little country—a quaint thing I could use to build a big dream."

"Nothing wrong with building big dreams," he says.

"True," I say. "But what I didn't realize is that you can't build big dreams off of little people or little places. If you're going to build a big dream, you have to have a big place. Maybe not literally, but a place with a big soul. And you have to have big people. Again, not literally," I say with a little smile. "But people with big hearts. I overlooked and underestimated the place and its people."

"You had your reasons," he says.

"I did," I reply. "But I didn't have to drag them all along with me."

"We drag a lot of things," he says. "Especially here in the country. Don't lose sleep over this. After all, you're a big lady yourself. Not literally," he says, winking. "And you'll do big things."

"Thank you," I say because it's the right thing to say, even though it feels all wrong. "I'm glad I got to know you."

"I'm glad I could help," he answers.

I'm not sure if he means with the house or with me figuring myself out. But whatever he means, it doesn't feel like enough, because he's about to turn and leave and I realize I don't want him to. I don't want his invoice in the mail. I don't want to hire some big company to do the work and have him not be there helping.

But even as I realize all these big things, it seems like he's had his own epiphany about me—one that doesn't match up with mine about him. Maybe I'm the one who's too country now. Or, more likely, the type of girl who lets big things go to her head, who can't appreciate the small things.

"I never did take you out to dinner," I say. "Some-time we'll have to cash in that raincheck."

"Aw, don't you worry yourself over that either."

He holds out a hand for me to shake. I don't want to shake his hand. I want him to wrap his arms around me, to surround me in his bigness—his bigness that I overlooked when I thought the country was too small for me.

Instead, I place my hand in his hand. He swings it up and down like we just sealed a deal, and he walks out the door. My door.

I'm standing alone in the kitchen, still staring at the door Jackson just walked out of, when I hear a tap at the front.

I step through the living area, the ash still in the fireplace, and unlatch the massive door. It sticks a little and I'm adding that to my mental list of things that will need to be fixed when the jammed door finally swings open, and I see a young man standing on my porch, his arms hooked over a pair of crutches.

"Can I help you?" I ask.

"Saw your car out back," the boy says, hopping in on his crutches like he knows me.

"Yes," I say, trying to be polite and figure out who

he is. Dirty blond hair, wiry frame, flying along on crutches.

And then it hits me. "Andy!" I say.

And before I can think of what else to say, he's wrapping me into a big hug.

"You're—" I begin. "Wow. I'm so glad you came over."

He spins a circle on his good leg. "Just wanted to stop by and say thank you now that I'm not all busted up and looking like a corpse. You shoulda seen Mama's face when she saw me."

"I can only imagine," I say. "It *is* good to see you fully conscious and with straight bones. How are you doing?"

He shrugs, the crutches staying down while his shoulders go up. "It's not my favorite thing in the world, but they got it fixed up real nice."

"I'm so glad." I usher him in, moving a blanket from the couch, so he can sit. "Come on in. I've still got some hot cocoa. I'll fix you some."

Jackson has stacked my remaining snacks in a little box in a pile with my paints. Seeing it there gives me a pang. I push it away as best I can.

The microwave hasn't arrived yet for the kitchen, so I fill the mug with water and hot chocolate mix and then head into Memaw's room for her microwave.

Andy whistles. "Kitchen looks real nice."

"Not bad, huh?" I say from the other room. "Jackson did that. Can you believe it? In one week."

"He's a busy man," Andy says. "Did you give him a chance?"

I come back into the room with the steaming hot chocolate. And maybe my smile is a little crooked, I don't know.

"Did you?" he asks again.

"I'm not sure he wanted a chance from me," I say, setting the cocoa down in front of Andy.

"Oh, I think he did," Andy says.

"Well you'll have to tell Jackson that, 'cause I just struck out pretty bad. Invited him to dinner and everything."

"My boy must be playing hard to get."

Another smile that must still be crooked. "I'm not sure he's playing," I say. "I don't think he wants to get caught, leastaways not by me." Somehow in the euphoria of seeing this kid that almost died spinning around on crutches, it's easy to let the country sink back in. And something about that feels good. Sitting in a parlor, with a hot drink, chatting it up.

"Maybe he's just afraid of getting caught."

"Hmmm," I say, wanting to change the subject.

Andy changes the subject for me. "Delicious," he says, tipping the cocoa back for the last few drops and standing to take his mug into the kitchen.

"I'll get it," I say, taking it from him before he can argue. "The first mug in my brand new sink."

"Thanks Ms. Bobbi," he says, and I freeze.

"What did you call me?" I ask, standing in the hole that is the wall, the mug dangling from my fingertips.

"Ms. Bobbi," he says, looking confused. "Would you rather I use your last name?"

"No," I say. "That's not it, it's just... No one's called me Bobbi for a long, long time."

"Oh," he says, like he's confused. "Mama said that was the name of Ms. Stephen's granddaughter. I was too out of it that night to remember your name, so I just asked Mama."

I turn to the sink. "Your Mama's not wrong. It's just a name I haven't used in a while. These days I go by Gretchen."

"That's real pretty too," he says.

"It's my middle name. Mama got it from a soap opera."

He laughs. "Better than a K Drama, I guess."

"Unlikely," I say.

He hobbles forward, using his crutches, and drops a little note on the end table. "Mama wanted you to have this. She sure appreciates everything you did for me."

I smile at him, walking into the living room and picking up the thick envelope. "Tell your mama I would have done it a thousand times over."

Andy smiles, then gives me a little salute. "Gotta tell me when your place is finished," he says. "I'm gonna give my girlfriend a tour."

"Didn't know you had a girlfriend," I say.

"Don't yet," he answers, "but with this leg, and the story, the ladies are falling all over me."

"Don't let it go to your head," I say. "You can't get in a life-threatening accident too often. So find you a girl who doesn't need a story or a wreck to make her swoon."

"I'll do my best," he says.

"And then bring her by," I finish, opening the door so he can get out with his crutches.

After all, it's about time *someone* brought a girl home to my memaw's house. Isn't that what grandparent's houses are supposed to be used for? Raising kids, making cookies, building families. So, yes, I think to myself, it's definitely time.

CHAPTER 20

One week later, Jackson's invoice comes in the mail. Which means that he's done with the wall as well. I find myself wishing I could go meet him there, inspect it, paint it together, something.

Instead, I pull out my brand new business checkbook with my brand new business name. Gretchen's Cottage. And write him a check. Less money than what he deserves for the quality of work.

I peek at the return address on the invoice, disappointed to see that it's a P.O. Box and not an actual physical address. I can't even stalk the man.

Not that I have the time.

I've spent at least half of the last week on the phone or the internet, ordering furniture, bossing around contractors, and arranging contracts with florists and caterers.

My to-do list is half a mile long. I still need furniture for all of the bedrooms. And if I want to refinish some of the pieces myself, I'm going to have to block out a few days to go down and do that. We'll be having an estate sale this weekend for the rest. Apparently there are companies who handle that sort of thing too, and I'm glad because the thought of a yard sale with all of Memaw's things might make me actually lose my mind.

I finger the sealed invoice with its pesky P.O. Box.

Since I can't properly stalk Jackson, I do the next best thing. I call his mother. It's not that she's the only real estate agent in Midvale. But she IS the only real estate agent in Midvale with a website, and that's kind of the same thing.

Her phone rings only once before she answers it, her voice with a swing of country, but tied up in a businesslike alto that I almost immediately like. "Hello, Mrs. Wilson. Your son, Jackson, gave me your name. I just inherited the old farmhouse out on Mill Road, and he mentioned that I might be able to rent out some of the farmland that came with it."

"Gretchen!" she says, like we're the oldest and

best friends in all the world. "Gretchen Stephens. Yes, he told me you might be calling."

Everything about that voice makes you feel both loved and confident at the same time. No wonder Jackson turned out like he did. "So," I begin. "How does it work?"

She explains it to me in basic layman's terms. "I imagine you're pretty busy, hon. With all that's going on right now at that house. And Jackson said you had a day job to boot."

"I do," I answer, resisting the junior high urge to ask if Jackson said anything else about me.

"Which means you're probably planning to stay up there in Swallowsville. Is that right?"

I can't help but feel that it's a loaded question. "Yes, ma'am. That's the plan."

She doesn't pause, doesn't miss a beat. "Okay, then you're probably going to want to have a property manager to handle the details. It won't be near as sticky as with a regular rental, but a property manager will handle any turnover, non-payments, things like that."

"For how much?"

"Usually about ten to fifteen percent of the rent. I'll have the property manager on my team call you."

"Any other costs?"

"With land there won't be too many. Taxes of course. Heaven knows you can't avoid those. You'll need to plan a good twenty percent to watch your back, more if your income gets too high."

"Well, right now that's not a huge problem."

"Just know that with that house and the land and your job, it could be. You want to have enough stashed away that Uncle Sam don't come and bite you in the backside."

"I certainly do," I say. "And with all that, do you think I'll turn a profit on the land, or will it be too much hassle to be worth it? Should I just let it lie fallow?"

"Oh honey, I think you'll turn a nice profit. You don't make near as much renting out land as houses, but you don't have much for overhead costs either. You don't have to repaint the place, or worse—gut it every time a bad renter leaves. You don't have to evict someone, well, not exactly. It's just easier. I'll have my property manager call you to talk about how much land you're looking at, and maybe we'll come out and have a look at it."

"That sounds great," I say. "I'm down at the house quite a bit on my days off—" I let that sentence hang there, hoping she's one of those moms who will get the hint, and shove her son back into my arms.

"Perfect," she says, and it suddenly doesn't seem like she *is* the type. At least not with me. "I'm sure we can work something out."

We both pause, and the good news is that I know she won't hang up on me. "How is Jackson doing after, uh, that stressful night?" I ask, fishing for a way to ask it that sounds normal and casual enough.

"Oh, he's good. He deals with stuff like that all the time at his work. 'Course being in a farmhouse with no electricity and a suffering patient isn't quite the same thing. But my boy's got a head on his shoulders."

"Yes, he did an amazing job," I say. "Please tell him that."

"I will," she says, a softness coming into her voice, along with just the breath of a pause. "After that night, when he was done with work he came home and slept for nearly a day and a half. Wouldn't take a single call from me. If I hadn't of known better, I would have thought he was sulking over something."

"I'm sure he was just so exhausted," I say carefully.

"I'm sure," she responds, also carefully. Then, "Between you and me, hon, that boy works himself half to death. Ever since his daddy died."

And to think that I had Jackson—this type A,

double job, loves-his-parents guy—pegged as a laid-back country boy working odd jobs.

"Thank you so much, Ms. Wilson."

"Call me Charlene. And don't you worry about renting that land. You won't regret it."

"Thank you," I say. "I believe I will rent it."

"Good. I'll send Jackson over sometime to make sure everything with your grandmama's house is on the up and up."

"Oh, you don't need to," I stutter. "Only if he wants to."

"Like I say," she says slyly. "I can't hardly get the boy to stop moving."

I put the phone down feeling slightly happy and also slightly deflated, and still slightly confused about why I couldn't make it right with Jackson.

Maybe there was never really any interest to begin with. Maybe I imagined it, or he and I got caught up in that strange night and then he woke up and realized, well, that it was just a strange night. I don't know. And I wish I did.

CHAPTER 21

INTERLUDE: JACKSON

I pull up to Mama's house after work. She texted me that she'd got a crockpot chili going and wants someone to eat it with.

Fair enough, though I'm still suspicious. Mama always has food for me when there's something on her mind.

And I've got a good guess what it is.

"Come on in, Baby," Mama says, dishes clanging like she's just a lady making supper, not a tiger about to corner her prey.

I sigh, then square my shoulders. The thing with Gretchen isn't that I'm not interested.

It's that she isn't, not really.

Not in the things that matter most to me. I want

fishing holes and lightning bugs, to sit outside at night and gaze at a sky full of stars. Thunderstorms, porch swings. I want my kids to grow up in the same town, to go to the same church I grew up in, to know everyone. I want that sense of connection and community I've known my whole life. That's why I'm here in Midvale.

Not because I had to be. As a nurse I could have gone just about anywhere, and for a few years after graduation, I did. Four years in the army to pay back my schooling. Then a stint in the Peace Corps as a way to pay back the world—to try to give a little of my good fortune to people who didn't have much. But when my dad died, I just wanted to be here. With my mama, and everyone else I loved.

When Gretchen started working on that house, all that light in her eyes, I thought she might see what I saw too, the potential in all of it, the beauty around us. And she did see the potential. And even the beauty. But not as a story's end. More as a stepping stone. To get her on to the next big thing. The next career move, up and up. Away and further away.

The house wasn't going to be a house. It was going to be a business. No night chats on the porch with lemonades. Just big parties with strangers and hired help to clean up afterwards.

Not that there was anything wrong with that. It's just that it isn't what I want, what I hope, for my life.

"She seems like a nice girl," Mama says, stepping into the dining room with a pot big enough to feed the whole state of Kentucky.

"You're not even going to let me sit down first," I respond, flopping into a chair and guzzling the water Mama's already put on the table. She sits across from me—both of us acting like we did when I was a teenager trying to get out of a conversation. "And she *is* nice," I add, filling a bowl without looking at her.

"Smart too," my mother says. "She asked all the right questions when she called me today." She dropped that bomb real casual.

"She called?"

"Of course. Asking about renting out the farm-land. Thinking upward, that girl."

"Well, you're welcome for the recommendation."

"She pretty?"

I sigh, setting down my bowl of chili. "Yeah."

"And?"

"She doesn't want to be here, Mama. It's not her home anymore. Truthfully, it sounds like it wasn't much of a home when she was here. But it's my home. And that's kind of a deal breaker."

"Lots of deal breakers in that brain of yours."

I roll my eyes, again just like a teenager.

"You know who that girl is?"

"Gretchen Stephens," I say sarcastically.

"Very good," Mama replies. "Grew up on Blue Hill where all them trailers used to be. Her daddy went to my school—a few years younger than me, thank the heavens. Because that boy was trouble. Oh, not at first. He could talk real sweet. In fact, he could talk his way into any girl's arms. Until he screamed and sometimes punched his way out. Wasn't a daddy in this town who liked that boy. But he played football, and had a real sweet face. He'd burned out nearly every option round here when Roberta moved to town—curvy and naïve. Just his style. She hadn't learned enough to stay away. They met right after graduation—the wrong time to meet the wrong boy in a small Kentucky town. They got married soon after. And your friend came along quite soon after that."

"Mama," I say, like it's none of my business.

"I'm just saying sometimes people have their reasons, and sometimes it's important to have a good look at them. Her daddy kept every bar in town in business until he died. People used to gossip that they'd kick him out at two and that the neighbors would hear him screaming till sunrise."

"It's not that I don't understand," I say. "It's just that it doesn't really matter. She doesn't want to be here, and I do."

"Which kind of shows how little you understand." Mama says. "She wants to be here enough to come down half the days she's off, fixing up that house, making it something that this town can be proud of."

"It's not because she wants the town to be proud. It's because she's invested in it as a business. And, I know—*ain't nothing wrong with that.*"

"How many people you know who've left this town who are willing to come back and fix up a house? After all, people have left. The Millers, Walkers, that Poulsen kid. They all had property they could have fixed. Could have gotten more money if they did. Called me and sold it without once setting foot on that land."

I sigh. "Fine, Mama. What do you want?"

"I think you oughta go back to her house, wish her well."

"I already did—and do—wish her well."

"Wish it better," she says.

CHAPTER 22

I didn't get the job.

No surprise there.

Still, I thought that maybe, just maybe…

But one line into the email, I can see what it is. "Thank you so much for your interest in the position at yada yada." And on it goes. I have to admit, I don't envy Jane, sending out those letters on the regular.

At the very end, she's included a little P.S. "Gretchen, I hope you consider us for future positions, maybe after some classes at the college. It was a very difficult decision."

I email back, real sweet. "Thank you for considering me. It was lovely to meet you, and I wish you the best."

CHAPTER 23

INTERLUDE: JACKSON

I wasn't going to do it. Wish Gretchen well. At least not in the way Mama intended.

I wasn't going to seek her out, go to the house like a little lost puppy, tell her how great I thought it all was.

Which isn't to say that I didn't wish her well, or even that I didn't think it was great—at least parts of it. Every time I drove past the house, it looked better. Freshly painted shutters, or new porch lights, or lanterns all along the walk to the front door. It hadn't exactly been an eyesore before, but it had looked like the sort of house where a grumpy older woman lived.

It didn't anymore. Now it looked like the type of

place you'd want to go, the type of place you might even want to walk down an aisle.

In fact, I keep my habit of driving by on my way to work. Which is kind of nonsensical since I'm going a couple miles in the wrong direction. But I keep driving it anyway, just to see all the new things that are happening.

Today, on my "way to work," there's a huge sign hung out front announcing an estate sale. People are lining up in the drive, following the bright signs to the front door and the barn out back. In fact, some people are already heading back to their cars with boxes of knickknacks or pieces of old furniture—her memaw's life getting hauled away by strangers.

I imagine doing that to my own granny, and it just feels too sad.

One lady has a large painting. I can't see if it's something personal or generic, but I avert my eyes anyway, drawing them back to the road.

And there, right in front of me, is a car that looks familiar. It swings into the drive, parking near the end, which is the only place with any space left. My minister hops out.

I slow, crawling past the house. Noticing me, he waves.

I wave back, stopping right on the road, and

rolling down my window as he trots back to greet me.

"Looks like you're the only one in town missing out," he says, nodding to the line of parked cars.

"Looks that way," I say, putting on my hazards, though no one is behind me on the road. In fact, every other car is turning into the drive, some of them now forced to park in the grass out front. Gretchen might have to lay a stretch of concrete to make a little parking lot, another fact I'm not a tremendous fan of.

"Why don't you come in for a spell?" Minister Howard asks.

I shake my head. "Nah, I've got to go…" I pause, realizing it will sound funny to say I have to go to work when I am two miles out of the way. So I just let my words hang in the air.

"Well, the missus is hoping I can find a few good antique lamps to go in our living room."

"I'd say you've got a decent chance," I reply.

"If all the good stuff isn't gone," he says.

"Get on then," I reply, beginning to roll up my window.

"See you Sunday," he says, waving as he jogs back to the drive.

I nod, though he surely can't see me.

A woman from the drugstore is getting out of her car, as well as Harry from the home store, a couple ladies from Mama's book club, and several flea market junkies.

There's something about it—all those cars lined up like the place was open for business. A little crack inside of me opens up. This is my community. And they *liked* what Gretchen was doing for it. And did Gretchen really have to keep all the stuff from a Memaw she'd never known, a Memaw who hadn't bothered to try to get to know her? But then again, did she have to get rid of it all?

The two sides have a little war inside of me. I'm not sure exactly which one wins, but I decide that I should probably send Gretchen a text or something —something small—a little congratulations.

After all, a country boy has to listen to his mama. And I still hadn't wished Gretchen well.

In the end, Gretchen beats me to it. Her own text pops up just as I'm leaving work that evening.

"I'm not sure you're interested in any more work on the house…"

She pauses in her texting and I wait.

"But I'm in a bit of a pinch. We had an estate sale today, and there are a few things I'll need to load into the trailer tomorrow. But everyone else I've called is booked."

Another pause.

"It'll only take a few minutes. I could pay you well for your time."

Something about the last line rubs me wrong. Is it all always about payment? But then, I wonder if maybe that's my own bias talking. After all, my actions from earlier weren't exactly a warm call-me-anytime-you-need-a-hand sort of thing. We've been on business terms. She's offering a business transaction.

So I guess the question is, do I want to accept it?

My finger hovers over the screen on my phone. I picture all those people, carrying out bits and pieces of her memaw's house. But then I just picture all those people, smiling, talking, heads bent together like they were having the best morning of their lives.

Mama's words hang in my head. "Wish it better."

What better way to wish her well than by helping this one last time?

I tell her she doesn't have to pay me.

CHAPTER 24

I wander through the house after the estate sale. I'd expected it to feel like this beautiful blank canvas, but instead it feels more like the empty cavern of a robbed tomb. Only the worthless items have been left behind—the things no one wanted.

Before the sale, I'd removed the pieces of furniture that I still wanted to redo, as well as any other things that looked like they might have a place on the shelves when the house gets finished. Plus an old wedding dress, which I'll probably end up consigning, but I wanted to have a little time to think about first. It's not like I've seen pictures with Memaw in the dress, not like I remember a specific dress or a pair of shoes or a favorite soft shirt. But there's something in the neat, careful way she'd hung it, along with all her things. I just wanted to keep *something*. The dress, along with the rest of the things I'm keeping are waiting neatly in Memaw's bedroom.

The rest of it is in a heap near the door. Though maybe heap isn't a fair word. Because the estate sale company was completely efficient and mercilessly meticulous. Every item is catalogued and boxed— from big to small.

On a whim I pick out a blue vintage dress from an open box. I'll add it to the wedding dress—my thinking pile, and put that in the shed as soon as the rest has been carted off.

For now, I walk along the remaining boxes— labeled with bright yellow stickers. These I have to decide what to do with. Donate, dump, burn? The estate sale company could have removed everything, discarded all the remaining items. Instead I asked them to box and leave what did not sell. An odd choice for me to make.

And one I might regret.

What is left behind are about ten large boxes, several mattresses, a broken dresser, and a cracked mirror that looks like it came straight out of a horror film. I don't dare look at myself in it. What if it sucks me up?

Jackson will be here any minute to help me load everything onto the trailer.

I wasn't going to ask him. I tried literally every other company I could think of including a random company on Facebook called Guys and Trucks. No one had time to come over on a Sunday, which is my day off. That left only Jackson.

I wish I felt excited to see him, but as his truck pulls up with the familiar rhythm, the dust kicking up behind it, I just feel nervous.

He arrives at my door, just like that first time. Flannel shirt, sturdy jacket, boots, hair tousled. Only this time I know he's really someone with more education and importance in the community than me, that this is just one of the many faces, the many skills, he's mastered.

"Hi!" I say, a little too brightly.

"Hey, Gretchen," he replies, not quite brightly enough.

"You ready for this?"

"Not sure I'm the one you should be asking," he says.

I blink. "Shouldn't take us too long. The hardest part will be the mattresses, so maybe we should start with those."

He glances at the trailer hitched to my vehicle.

"You might want to end with them actually. They'll act as a natural sort of "tarp" to keep the other stuff weighted down."

"Okay," I say, feeling a little dumb about it all.

"You've got rope to tie it down?" he asks.

I hold out the nylon ties.

"Nice," he says as we head into the house, through the beautiful kitchen, which is now open to the living space.

"You did a great job," I say.

"Thank you," he answers, pausing to observe his own work. "It really does look good. And you chose the perfect materials, a beautiful color palette."

"I did," I say. "Palettes are my specialty."

He laughs. It's a nice sound. I sit in it for a second, feeling the echoes of it against the mostly empty walls.

"Most of it's in the front room," I say, leading him there.

The room is stacked with the boxes, the broken furniture, the creepy mirror. "So where *should* we start first?"

"Boxes probably," he says, looking around. "Then that spooky mirror. Hopefully it's not possessed or something."

"That's what *I* thought," I say. "Why do you think I hired you? I can't even look at it."

"So you want me to get sucked in, not you."

"I mean, I didn't want to say so over the phone…" I answer.

It's then that I realize we're standing close—closer than I thought we were, closer than we were a minute ago—and we're smiling into each other's faces, his head tipped down, a piece of hair falling across his forehead.

I have to step back to stop myself from reaching up and moving it away.

"We'll put that between the boxes," he says, pointing to the mirror, "and under the mattresses." He pulls a sheet off one of the mattresses and drapes it over the mirror. "There."

"Better," I say.

"Have you gone through the boxes?" he asks. "Made sure there wasn't anything you wanted?"

"I took what I wanted before they came," I say, glancing at the boxes, wondering if I should go through them one final time.

He nods with a thoughtful look I can't quite read. Then says, "Okay, let's get 'er done."

I nod.

Most of the boxes are light—full of broken trinkets, clothes, and old makeup. I catch Jackson reading the boxes like he thinks I'm throwing away valuable heirlooms.

The last three boxes are full of heavier stuff—used blankets and a few pictures that didn't sell. I can't lift them on my own. And even if I could, I doubt the boxes would hold.

"These are going to have to be unboxed," I say, opening one as Jackson comes in. The box is labeled pictures. It should be just generic things, since I thought I'd set all the family portraits aside.

I was wrong.

Gazing back at me from the top of a stack of flea market art is a full portrait I've never seen before—a portrait with my daddy's name on the back. Eighteen or nineteen years old. Staring at it, I find the high forehead I remember, the swish of dark blond hair, the take-all smile with a crooked eyetooth on the left. Plus all the swagger in the world.

But that's not what stops me.

"What?" Jackson says, as I cover the picture with the flaps of the box, slumping onto the floor in front of it.

"How long ago did my Daddy leave this house?" I say, half to myself, half to Jackson.

"I don't know. Maybe as soon as he finished high school."

"He married my mama and they moved to the trailer on the outskirts—the place where I grew up."

"Okay," Jackson says, coming over and gently opening the box. I let him. He lifts the picture out, staring at it, just like I did. It's huge, a fancy portrait.

"How old were you when he died, Gretchen?"

"Seven, almost eight." I nod to myself, then mutter, "So the ages don't line up."

He clears his throat.

"What?" I say.

"Nothing," he responds. "It's a nice picture of your dad. Are you going to keep it?"

"Don't you see it?" I ask.

He looks at it again, and I know he does. I can tell from the tight clench of his face, the lines of his forehead, crushing toward each other.

That picture is the spitting image of Andy—a boy who several weeks ago was casually riding around on my memaw's property.

"Did he have any brothers, my dad?"

"I mean, I'm not an expert on this town, Gretchen—you'd probably know better about your family than I would—but I don't think he did."

"So I can't have any cousins," I murmur. "And I

should know better, but you'd be surprised how little I know, and with everyone gone, it's kind of hard to find out."

"He maybe had second cousins or something," he says. "You'll have to dig in to your family history."

"Right," I say. "Of course. And who *is* Andy's daddy?"

"Gretchen, I know it's a little town, but I really don't know *everything* about everybody."

"But it would have been on his hospital work," I answer. "Right?"

"Not necessarily," he says. "Andy wasn't a minor. He could sign himself in."

"But his mama came to the hospital," I say.

"Of course."

"And his daddy?"

"I didn't see him. If he's even got a dad at home. His parents could be divorced, or never married."

On the last phrase, I want to shush Jackson, tell him not to be stupid. Instead, I just nod. Keep nodding, like it's the only thing my body can do.

"I'll have to look up his dad," I say. "See if he's connected to my daddy. Because the ages don't line up, so it'd have to be a second cousin, or maybe just a weird coincidence. Maybe just an uncanny resemblance."

But I know it's not. I cleaned every inch of that face—Andy's face—swabbing up dried blood, tending to the cuts that were still bleeding. I saw it, the curve of his cheeks, the color of his eyes, the brows arching up.

I only remembered my daddy as old, as broken—his skin like leather, yellow teeth, some of them broken and rotting in his mouth. I didn't remember this, this portrait, this youth. Though just a few weeks ago, I'd seen it. Seen it in a boy that we'd dragged into this house on a homemade sled. Seen it in a face I'd cleaned of blood, seen it in that crooked tooth, in this swaggering smile. The two young faces cut from the same cloth as only relatives could be.

"That would be wild if Andy was related to me," I say, taking the portrait from Jackson's hands. "For this weird minute, I thought, well, it doesn't matter —the ages don't line up; he's just a teenager. But they're spitting images of each other. Isn't that the wildest thing? Small town Kentucky," I say, smiling up at Jackson.

He's not smiling back. "Gretchen," he finally says, his mouth moving slowly, his whole body moving slowly as he takes the picture from my hands. "How was it that your daddy died?"

"Drunk or suicide," I answer. "Not that there's much difference when you drank like Daddy did."

Jackson presses his lips together, setting the portrait gently on the top of the box. "I don't really know if I'm allowed to tell you this because of HIPAA and stuff, though I figure it's common enough knowledge, but Andy wasn't a teenager. I know he looks young, but he's twenty-four, almost twenty-five."

"Twenty-four?" I ask, sitting there, glad I'm not still holding the picture. "No."

"Yes," Jackson says. "*Almost* twenty-five."

I shake my head. "What are you saying?"

"I'm not *saying* anything," Jackson says. "Only how old Andy is. You thought he was eighteen or nineteen, but it's not true."

True. What a word. I try to wrap my brain around it, around this boy that looks just like my young father, around my grandmother's house only a few miles from that boy—that boy who was allowed free rein on her property, property that I myself had never seen until she died.

The pieces of truth mix together until they click. My daddy drinking every night, doing who knows what every night, my parents fighting every night. Every night. Every morning. Until that morning.

When Daddy was dead. The mud on his boot the shape of Florida. Mud, or blood? I don't know, because even in a town where everyone knows every single piece of everyone else's business, not a single person could tell me, would tell me, the truth about how my daddy died.

Or maybe why my daddy died—his life taken through the poison of that much alcohol, or a shot that ended it quickly. But taken by his own hand one way or another. For one reason. Or another.

Perhaps a reason I had never considered.

A fight between him and Mama I had never thought to imagine. Another woman, sure, that was one thing. But another child? That was a whole other argument.

I push past Jackson, heading toward the entrance that was once a wall. Jackson takes my arm, stops me. "Gretchen," he says. "There could be a thousand explanations for the resemblance."

"Did you know?" I ask Jackson, swirling around toward him in the room where we cared for Andy all through that snowy night. "Did this whole stupid town know?"

I feel the hot tears on my cheeks, shake them off. Jam my palms against my face, trying to cool my cheeks, trying to calm the swell rising up in me.

He shakes his head. "*If* what you think is true…"

I glare at him. "You think it too."

"*If* what *we* think is true, then I don't know if anyone knows, or knew. Besides maybe your memaw," he says, gesturing to the box with the picture. "And Andy's mom, I suppose."

"I suppose," I say, wrapping my confusion and anger and hurt up deep inside myself. "Would you get the mirror? I'll repack those boxes while you do, so we can carry them."

"Gretchen, maybe we should stop for the day. Revisit this later in the week."

"It's my only day off," I say matter-of-factly. "And would you please tell your mother I'd like to meet with her about selling the house?"

"Selling?" he says.

"This town cut me off years ago," I say. "I was silly to think there was a place for me, for the person I was, and definitely not for the person I've become."

"If what you think is true," he begins.

"Say the words," I say more harshly than I mean to. "If Andy is my half-brother."

"Okay. If Andy is your half-brother, then you have *more* connection to this town, more reason to stay."

"Oh, please," I say. "You never wanted me to keep

this house anyway, not if I was going to make it a business."

"It's your homestead," Jackson says, holding my shoulders and looking into my eyes.

I shake his hands off. "It's no more my homestead than a parrot in Alaska. We don't belong together, me and this house. Me and this town. I thought maybe we could. I thought maybe I could come back —not as that broken little girl, but as me, the full me, bring something of myself here. But nothing in this town is going to want that. Not you—" I say, seeing that he's trying to interrupt. "Not Andy's mama, who's clearly been keeping a very big secret for a very little town. Not anyone."

"Sometimes people keep secrets because they don't know what else to do with them," he says, stealing another glance at the picture.

"Maybe that's true, and I don't hold her any kind of a grudge. But that's a whole lot of secrets and a whole lot of baggage for me to come back to."

"If it's baggage, then unpack it," Jackson says. "Talk to Andy. Talk to his mother. Work things out."

"Work things out?" I ask. "Like that I inherited all this land, this house, a place worth quite a bit of money really. And he got nothing."

"Talk to him."

"If Andy *is* my half-brother, he deserves half of this house. And I can't afford to buy him out."

"The house is yours, Gretchen. It was given to you. That's just the law."

"Well, I'm giving half of it back," I say. "That can be the law too."

"What about the people in your Kickstarter?" Jackson asks.

I'm surprised he remembers. "I can refund them the money, issue an apology."

"Gretchen," he says.

"Circumstances have changed," I say. "That's how I'll word it. Now can you get that mirror? I don't think we need to worry about it being possessed anymore. Not when this whole old house is."

I've given myself the day off to sulk and sit and eat ice cream—normal sorry-for-myself things.

So when the bell rings, I'm expecting the pizza I ordered, or maybe a package with more lipstick samples. Bits of my regular, predictable, and perfectly normal life.

I'm not expecting Andy—in a neat collared shirt and nice jeans—to show up at my house, flowers in hand.

"Oh, hey," I say.

He hands me the flowers—thrusts them really, right into my hands.

"Thank you."

"I heard you was my sister."

And I can't help it. At the absolute bluntness, I smile. "Half-sister, I guess."

"Yeah, that's what Mama said."

"That's why she knew my name," I murmur, looking down at the flowers. They're nice—really nice. Roses mixed in with delicate branches that have red berries. And strewn among all the red, instead of something usual like baby's breath, there are these silver and green sprigs of something that smells nice. Eucalyptus. "My old name."

"I like your new name," Andy says.

"It's always been my name," I say. "Just not my first name. Course Bobbi wasn't either. Roberta is my actual first name. Same as Mama's."

"I know," he says.

"I guess Jackson went over and talked to you."

"Well, not exactly. More like he called my mama. You know how it goes. And then there was this whole lot of squealing. Happy, sad, mad. All the squealing. And then, Mama handed me the phone and Jackson went on, and told me my mama had something she had to tell me, and she said she didn't want to, and Jackson told me to just wait. So I did. It took an hour, and Jackson waited on the phone that whole time, while Mama cried."

"Whoa," I say.

And Andy, he laughs. "You have no idea."

"I mean, I have a little idea," I say. "I'm *from* Midvale, you know. And not nearly as respectable a part as you. We did more than squeal at my house."

"Not so respectable as you thought I was though."

And now it's my turn to laugh. "You are every bit as respectable as I thought," I say. "Though at least years older."

"Mama said she was sorry," he says.

"She doesn't have to be sorry," I say. "How old was she when she met my daddy? Eighteen?"

"Pretty close," he answers.

I shake my head. "How old?"

"Sixteen."

I blow out a long breath. Then pause. That would make his mother just eight years older than me, and younger than Macie. "Your poor mama."

"Ah, now, she's doing alright. She works at the Family Dental Center downtown."

"Hygienist?" I ask.

Andy smiles. "Not quite."

"Reception?" I say.

He smiles bigger, and I see those white, clean teeth, even though the eyetooth *is* a bit crooked.

"Dentist," he says.

My mouth opens just a bit. "Oh," I say. "I'm so

sorry. I just…" *Assumed.* Again. Single mom, teen pregnancy, small town Kentucky, couldn't possibly be a dentist.

"She told me she woulda killed me if I'd gone and knocked my teeth out on 'that thing'—that's what she calls my four wheeler."

"I bet she does. So, did she remarry?"

"You mean marry the first time," Andy says with a laugh. "There was no 're-' to do. And, no. She always said I kept her too busy."

"I mean, she probably wasn't wrong," I say with a smile.

"Not at all," he says. "My greatest accomplishment was keeping her on her toes."

"Looks like you're still at it," I say. "Does she know you're here?"

He doesn't answer. "She didn't know it was you that helped me that night, not at first. Though she eventually put it together of course. Seems like now it's her turn to keep me on my toes."

"Did you know that Ms. Stephens was your memaw?"

"We had to eat there once a month, Sunday. But, no, I didn't know. Crazy small town stuff, huh?"

Now it's my turn not to answer. "You find you that girlfriend yet?"

"Too many choices," he answers.

"Well, don't break all those hearts," I answer, feeling an uncomfortable pang. *Don't be your father.*

"And what are your plans?" I ask, done making assumptions. "Dentist? Doctor? Engineer?"

"I want to own an ATV shop in town, sell the things I love."

I am not winning at the assumptions game. "You should definitely do the things you love."

"That's what they say. Mama is going to give me a loan to get started. Says I have to pay her back every year. We went through the numbers, worked it out. I'm pretty alright with numbers, not as much a fan of words."

"About that—numbers," I say. "I might be able to help out."

Andy holds up a hand to stop me. "Jackson said you were thinking of selling the house."

"Not thinking of," I answer. "That's what I've decided to do. When I do, I can give you half. It only seems fair."

"Does it?" he asks, sitting on the couch beside me.

"Of course," I answer, confused.

"Yeah," he says. "Only child. Raised by a single mother. In the deep hills of Kentucky. That kind of kid deserves a financial boost, right?"

"Yes," I answer. "That's what I'm trying to say."

"Well, I wasn't that kid," he answers. "I was raised for at least half my life in Lexington, while Mama went to dental school and my grandmamma watched me. Her husband, my granddaddy, he raised race horses out there, made good money from it—better than good. Helped Mama through school."

"But why did she move back to Midvale?" I ask. "What was there for her in that place?"

"A really good job," he answers. "A place she could start her own practice for a fraction of the price as in Lexington, and with no competition whatsoever. The previous dentist, he was retiring. She got his building—and with it, his clientele—for a song. And they loved her."

"And no one knew," I said. "Her story."

"They didn't even realize where I'd come from," he said with a grin. "Neither did I, to be honest. Until yesterday."

"But how was she there in the first place?" I ask. "When she, uh, met my daddy."

"She was hitchhiking her way across the country and got a little side-tracked. And, apparently, a lot drunk."

"I'm sorry," I say.

"Don't be," he answers. "She says it was the thing

that shook her awake. She went back home, got her life together. And here I am. Raised in a loving home. With good business sense like my grand-daddy, a good brain from my mama. And maybe a bit of a wild streak from the daddy I never knew."

I raise my eyebrows.

"But not too wild," he says. "Just a little wilder than dental school."

I laugh. "That doesn't take *too* much wildness."

"That's what I tell Mama."

"Well, I'm glad it didn't ruin you, my daddy," I say. "Well, our daddy."

"He never had a chance," Andy replies. "Unlike someone else I know."

I tip my head to the side, look at him like I'm a bird.

"Only child. Raised by a single mother. In the deep hills of Kentucky. That kind of person deserves a financial boost."

I shake my head, seeing where he's going. "It's not right," I say.

"Mama said Ms. Stephens came to her asking for money when she got old. Mama refused. But someone sent money. Who was it, Gretchen?"

I look at him.

"Nope. Not the wealthy dentist."

"She didn't owe Memaw a thing," I say.

"That's what she said. But you didn't owe your Memaw a thing either."

I look down into my lap. The flowers are still there—a little bundle of red and glitter.

"Keep the house, Gretchen. It's yours fair and square. On all levels. On all counts."

I tilt my head back, roll my shoulders. "It isn't right," I say.

"You mean, it ain't right," he answers. "That's how we say it down in Midvale. And since you're going to be coming home and opening shop, you ought to learn the lingo. And you're right—it ain't right—me robbing the house from you when you've had every disadvantage. And when you legitimately saved me when I was legitimately trespassing on your property."

"You didn't know any better," I say.

He gives me a flat stare. "Gretchen, I'm almost twenty-five and about to open my own business. I think I knew better."

"Besides, Jackson was the one who saved you."

"You both did," he answers. "Together."

"Mmm," I say, leaning back. "How much land do you think is that out there?"

"I don't know," he says. "Reckon about twenty acres."

"You reckon pretty close to correct," I say. "Twenty-four. How about we split it? You get twelve."

He looks me in the eye, and in that moment, I see it, our sameness, our stubbornness. "Mama said you were going to rent it."

"We could split that," I answer.

"Half and half ain't fair," he says.

I lean forward. "Seems pretty fair to me. Look, Andy, I want you to have some of your rightful inheritance, so tell me what *you* think is fair."

He taps his chin. "Truth is, I think you keeping it *is* fair."

"But I don't," I interrupt, "so think more."

He presses his lips together before answering. "There is a stretch that's fun to ride. Might even be fun enough to rent out ATVs and make some money. What do you think? A few acres of shared land. You own it still—" He holds up a hand to keep me from arguing back. "—But I'm allowed to use it for free. People pay to rent my ATVs, ride on your property. We split the profits, and both win."

"Not split the profits," I say. "You keep eighty percent."

"Sixty," he replies.

"Seventy," I say.

He nods, holds out a hand.

I take it. "I'll call a lawyer in the morning."

"A surveyor too," he says. "We want it all nice and clear, laid out real solid, so no one gets miffed as the years go by."

"That's how you do the best business," I say.

"I'll call the surveyor," he answers.

"Nice doing business with you, Andrew Patterson."

"Pleasure's all mine," he says, hitting my back in a very brotherly way. "And I guess now I'll be having dinner with *you* once a month, Sundays."

"I'd like that," I say, looking into his face. He's still got a few scars from the accident, from wounds I helped seal. "I can't believe I have a brother."

"And you thought you were going to get away with being all orphaned and lonely for the rest of your life," he says with a smile.

"I thought Midvale didn't have anything to hold me."

"Well," he answers with that wild twinkle in his eye. "If you look around, you might find it's got more than just a little half-brother to keep you company."

"I see what you're trying to do," I say. "And even if I wanted it to work, it wouldn't."

He shrugs. "We'll see." He turns to the door. "Oh, the flowers by the way, they're from Jackson."

I sit on the couch after he leaves, not moving, barely breathing. Like my body is a thing apart from the rest of me, apart from time, apart from feelings.

And then my phone pings. And again. And again.

Another appointment, another bill, another reservation in need of scheduling and detailing. I don't have time to sit and ponder the deep and bizarre connections of the world. I have a business to run.

CHAPTER 26

INTERLUDE: JACKSON

Gretchen's not selling the house. No sign. No call to my mama to put it on the market.

I slow my car to look at the beautiful old farmhouse. One more month and Gretchen would be ready for her first event.

It wasn't much time.

Which *could* explain why she hadn't called. I look away from the house. Of course the other thing that could explain it was that she wasn't interested. Not in touching base. Not in saying hello. Not even in asking for help. Maybe it's too much with a new brother and a new business and a new town. Maybe she didn't want to add a new man as well. Fair enough.

I pull into the little Italian restaurant run by people from Tennessee, and glance around to see if Mama is already there. She's not.

Which gives me a second. I glance down at my phone, at the message I just received last night. Real late. I'd called back as soon as I'd gotten it. And the news wasn't good. It never was that late at night. I click back to my thread with Gretchen. No new message I've missed. Nothing.

That made it easier at least. To make the choice.

Mama comes in and I lean down to give her a hug.

"You gonna go?" she asks before we've even taken our seats.

"Seems like the right thing to do," I say.

She nods softly. "Poor little thing. I'm glad you're wanting to go. But what about your job?"

"I've got a bunch of time saved up—you know I never take vacation. Plus a few weeks of bereavement."

"They gonna count bereavement for a sick friend?" she asks.

"I talked to the director and she said we could."

The server sets down breadsticks with water. "Bring me a Diet Coke, if you don't mind," Mama says. When she turns back to me, it's with an intentionally blank face. I've seen it a million times when she's about to ask a question she thinks might be touchy. "And what about that house, Gretchen's house—you all caught up?"

"I been caught up for weeks," I say, looking out the window as the server sets Mama's Coke down, glancing between us to see if we're ready to order.

"One more minute," Mama says.

He scurries away.

"And no new jobs?" she asks. "On the house?"

"I think Gretchen's calling it a cottage," I reply. "That's what the website says."

"Don't try to distract me from the subject," she replies.

I look her in the eyes. "No new jobs. Not since we cleaned it out."

"You sure you want to go out of town?" Mama asks, leaning forward, touching my hand. "It's such a long trip."

I take her hand, wrapping her little fingers into mine.

"I want to do it for Essie. She and Haley were such good friends."

"Like sisters," Mama says, squeezing my hand.

What we don't say is that now it feels like

another piece of Essie—her best friend—is dying too.

"Just don't stay away too long," Mama murmurs.

"I couldn't stay away from this town if I tried," I answer. "It always pulls me back."

"Good," she says, just as the waiter pops up again.

"Well, darn it all," Mama says, opening her menu. "Aren't we just a couple of slow pokes?"

"Speak for yourself," I say. "I want the meatball trio."

Mama sighs. "Oh, to be young. Give me the Caesar salad, hun."

When he's gone, Mama looks at me, real deep and serious in the eyes. "Promise me you'll take advantage of being young."

"Mama," I say.

"Promise me you'll try."

CHAPTER 27

$\mathcal{I}$ finally dropped a thank you for Jackson in the mail. The flowers, Andy, his family. Everything. I wrote it out by hand. But it still didn't seem like quite enough. Especially now that it's been a few weeks. But I think…I think I'm ready now.

To see him again, to thank him in person.

I put on my slimmest jeans, a red sweater that slips off one shoulder. Not practical with the temperatures we've had, but pretty. I even put on a pair of silver pumps. Not too much, but well, a little…extra.

And then I make my way to his mother's office, bold as anything. I start out by asking how she's doing (it's rural America, after all—you can't skip all the niceties), and then ask if she knows if he's home. I'm planning to ask her for his address if he is.

"Oh, honey," she says. "He'll be gone for a while. Got a piece of bad news a week ago. From one of his sister's sweet little friends. Friend of the whole family to be honest. He had to fly out to California for a bit. You know how he is, always doing things for those closest to him."

I did know this, knew it well. In fact, he did nice things for everyone, even me. Why wouldn't he do something for an old family friend? His sister's friend. His sister's friend, whom he was willing to fly across the country to meet. Which sounded kind of like more than just his sister's friend.

"Oh," I say. "I hope she's okay."

"Well, you keep hoping, darlin', because she isn't doing well. They found some cancer. Real late. Probably too late. He thought that with his skills he could…well, he could nothing, but he wanted to be with her in her last days. It's kind of a lot after Essie's passing. Those girls—just kids. Have mercy, it's definitely too much." And then she tears up.

"I'm…" I begin, looking around for a tissue box. "Wow. I'm so sorry."

And I am. How awful to have someone you care about be close to death. After your own sister died.

I locate the tissues, grab her one.

"Thank you, sweetheart," she says, dabbing at her eyes.

"I'll just, uh, I'll just text him then."

"You do that, honey. I'm sure he'd love to hear from you while he's there." Charlene is making quick work of the tissue, and I hand her another. "It would mean the world to him."

I smile—like there's anything else to do. Yeah, I'm sure he'd be thrilled to hear from me while he's with an old flame who is dying from cancer. Just years after his own sister died in an accident.

I glance at the door.

"Thanks for letting me know, Charlene."

"Anytime, honey. You come on over any time."

I mean to text him right away. I'm not a monster, after all, and this woman is dying right under his nose.

But as my fingers hover over my phone, I start to wonder. I mean, someone he cares about is dying. And he flew all the way out there to see her. Should I really be bugging him and asking how he is, and if things are alright, when it's pretty clear that they're not? Do I really want to be that type of an interruption? A mildly desperate-looking interruption.

No, I tell myself, putting my phone away. They need time; he needs time. And he deserves it.

Plus, I'm insanely busy. At the house almost every possible non-working moment—refinishing the furniture, discussing blueprints with Andy, calling caterers, and making plans for the official grand opening. December 20th. The weekend before Christmas.

The grand opening is the perfect distraction. Except that every time I walk into the kitchen, I think of him. When the new refrigerator arrives (finally) I think of him helping me haul that disgusting old fridge out of the house. I think of him when I hear a truck coming up the driveway. And every time I light the fire.

It's on one of those nights that it's gotten late and it's gotten cold and I've decided to sleep in the house and then drive back for work in the morning. One of those nights where my thoughts wake me in the middle of the night and then keep me awake. One of those nights when I pad out to the gorgeous fireplace with the slate accents just like he suggested. One of those nights (or maybe now it's morning) that I'm lighting the fire—still using that same box of matches that he found in the shed—one of those nights that a thought trickles to me.

Maybe.

Maybe after he's had time to heal. After I've gotten the business up and running. Maybe when we're both in a better place, a newer place.

Maybe.

It's a maybe that kind of feels good. Like a light before the sun comes up.

***

The next day I do text him, thank him for the flowers, for ironing things out with Andy's family like he did.

"Gretchen!" his text comes through. "It's so good to hear from you!"

"I'm so sorry to hear about your friend," I text back. "Your mama told me. How is she doing?"

"You wouldn't believe it," he texts.

"I'm so sorry," I begin.

"No," he texts. "She's doing amazing; she might even pull through."

"Oh," I reply. "Wow."

"It's like one of those miracles on a movie. The doctors are just blown away."

"That's...." my finger hovers over the phone, "so great," I text. "I'm really happy for you."

"Thank you, Gretchen. As soon as she's well enough I'm planning to fly her home so she can see Mama."

"Oh," I text. "Your mama would love that. She got weepy talking about it."

"Well, that's Mama for you. She loved Haley."

I pause, looking at the phone. "I'm so happy for you," I text again.

It's not a lie. It's just that suddenly I'm a little less happy for me.

"Sorry, gotta go," he texts. "She's calling."

⸻

My phone rings—the number somewhat familiar though I can't place it.

I let it ring through the first time. Probably just a spammer or something. But when the call comes again, I take it, planning to tell them to take me off their call list. I don't want them harassing me all night.

And then, Jane's voice. Something about the other candidate falling through. And I was next on the list. Would I still be interested in taking the job? If so, they would love to have me.

I can barely process it.

"The job?" I ask.

"Yes," Jane says. "If you haven't accepted another."

I clear my throat. "No, uh, I haven't."

"But I need to tell you…" She pauses, and I get a sticky feeling in my gut. Reduction in salary? Longer hours? More travel?

"We've made some changes to our structure and will need you to be onsite more than originally intended."

"Onsite?" I ask.

"Yes," she says. "In our Louisville office. We want you here unless you're travelling. You'll be doing most of your work from this office."

"So it's not remote?" I ask, trying to wrap my mind around it.

"I'm afraid it's not," she answers.

"I'll be in Louisville all week?"

"Correct."

"Would I still have my weekends?" I ask.

"Of course," she answers.

Weekends were enough time to see my friends. Weekends were enough time to run the Cottage. Not quite the same as I'd anticipated, but sufficient. As for Andy, well, I promised him Sunday dinners, and that could still work. In fact, with him as a business partner, it could work even better. I could probably pay him to manage some of the things that I would have done if I'd still been in Swallowsville. We could chat about it Sundays over a fat roast. At Memaw's house. No, not Memaw's house, I remind myself. My house. Or, at least Gretchen's Cottage. My business. What better place to eat and chat and work with Andy?

Any other reason for staying close to Midvale had flown off to meet a woman in California.

"I know this is a bit sudden," Jane is saying.

"I'll take it," I say, cutting her off. "I'm thrilled for the opportunity."

Jane pauses. "I expect you'll need some time to find a house here. So we'll keep the position hybrid for another month or so. Let's shoot for having you here onsite for the new year."

"The new year," I echo.

Perfect.

New year, new life.

Time to grab the opportunity that's actually staring me in my face instead of daydreaming about maybes.

CHAPTER 28

The weeks to December fly by in a whirlwind—a brutal, cold, dizzying whirlwind. Orientation, business calls, trips to different stores in the tristate area. Learning my job, the paperwork—ugh, all the paperwork. Is that what my life is going to look like now? But there's no time to think about that.

The house still needs work. But even when I hear I hear Jackson is back in town, I let him be. When I come down to work on the house or look for furniture, I don't let him know I'm there. When I need help with wiring, I call someone else, even though it means I have to delay the repair. When I'm wondering about stain colors, I figure it out myself. The old Gretchen way. Alone.

It's not that I don't want to contact him. It's how much I do that scares me.

I sign up for my classes, find an apartment in Louisville that has an opening mid-January. It's not as cute as my Swallowsville apartment, and nothing at all like Memaw's house, but I remind myself that it doesn't have to be, because within six months I should have enough saved for a down payment for a house.

I notice that I'm reminding myself about money a lot these days—every time I log in at work, every time a new order form comes, every time I'm asked to deal with complaints and problems and shortages in the different stores. Even the travelling, which I thought would be fun, is exhausting—walking into a store with a bunch of strangers, many of them not at all happy to have me there, telling them how to do their jobs.

My shoulders hurt almost permanently and I've started sleeping poorly. But on those nights when I'm lying awake wondering how it will all pan out, I remind myself how fat that first paycheck was, how far I've come from a trailer park in Blue Hill. I remind myself that in a few years I'll be a college graduate.

Although sometimes, very late at night, my mind

—traitor that it is—asks why I'm doing this for a couple pieces of paper, whether it's a college degree or more Benjamin Franklins than I ever thought I'd hold in my bank account.

CHAPTER 29

The tree is half decorated, meaning Becca's boyfriend, Lance, has managed to get the lights around it. At almost ten feet tall, it was no small feat.

Now the rest of us dive into boxes of decorations —most of them old things I pulled from Memaw's attic, though I've added several bags of other vintage ornaments, along with a few modern beauties.

The Christmas tree will either look like trailer trash, or like it came from a 1950s Sears catalogue. I'm going for the latter.

And we don't have much time. Within hours, our first guests will be arriving for the open house.

This event—it's my gift (plus advertisement—let's

be honest) to the community. Something fun that will show them what Gretchen's Cottage has to offer.

Lance is still on lights duty, working his way around the porch. Macie, Becca, and I are frantically pulling decorations from the ancient tissue paper that turns to dust in our hands.

Tad sneezes. "Okay, what's my job?" he asks.

"Hot cocoa," Macie answers before I can tell him not to worry about it.

"Homemade?" he asks.

"Of course," I reply. "It's one part cocoa, two parts sugar, four parts milk. You'll find everything but the milk on the counter."

"And the *hors d'oeuvres*?" he asks.

"The caterers should be here soon," I say. "So if you can get the hot cocoa, coffee, and water for tea ready, we can put them in the carafes." I'm sweating, just saying it, thinking about it. Tables are set, all the other décor is up. But I wanted to wait until my friends got here to do the tree. Doing it alone in this old house—no matter how new it looks—well, I just didn't want to.

Becca holds a pink vintage ornament up to the light. "Do I love it or hate it?" she asks.

"Love," I say.

"You didn't even look," she replies.

"Time," I answer, feeling the beads of sweat along my forehead.

Becca steps in front of me. "Deep breaths," she says. "The place looks gorgeous, everything is ready, the food will be here soon. Now tell me if this is pretty or not." She holds the rose-colored ornament up to my face.

It is decidedly pretty, in that old fashioned way of very old things. Minimal scratches too. I glance at the tree. "Yes," I say. "Pretty. And a good match. In fact, maybe we can try to keep everything to these rose colors with some darker mauve and silver."

I look around. It needs an accent of some sort as well. Not red or green. "And navy," I say. "Dark navy."

"Like this?" Macie says, holding up a tatted...something.

"Um," I say. "It's the right color."

Macie laughs. "Okay. Right color. Wrong thing."

"Snowflake," Becca shouts.

I glance outside nervously. There's a chance of it in the forecast—not a storm or anything—but I'm still a little nervous.

"No, here," she says, holding up a beautiful navy snowflake with white and silver accents.

"Yes," I say. Then, "Has anyone seen Andy?"

"Outside," Tad says, making his way slowly into the room with a shot glass of cocoa for Macie to try. "What do you think?" he asks.

"Perfect," she says.

I glance at them and they're smiling—not just into each others' faces, but a whole body smile as they lean toward each other. I look away. "So he's out back?"

"Yup," Tad says. "Making a racket."

Andy has created a path through several acres of woodland, as well as a sort of parking area where people will leave their cars and get their ATVs. We've got a little barn there, where they'll be stored.

I also helped walk him through the process of insuring them as well as getting releases so he doesn't get sued. Both of which endeared me a bit to his mother, whom I kind of like. She is—as Becca would say—Girl Boss Extraordinaire. A title Becca has also begun applying to me.

I pause to listen to Andy's 'racket'—which I can't hear nearly as well as Tad probably can. Then say, "Music. Shoot."

"I got it," Tad says.

And he does. Classical-sounding Christmas pipes through the house.

The tree is starting to glisten and just as I open my mouth to say so, the lights on the porch all come on. Like a shower of glitter. We all pause, take a collective breath.

And then, I can't help it. The tears spring to my eyes before I can stop them.

Macie and Becca stop, surround me in that little circle women make. I wave my hands. "It's okay," I say. "It's just so…so…"

"Beautiful," Becca says.

"Magical," Macie adds.

"Glorious," I finish.

"It's a season for angels, after all," Becca says. "I'm just hoping a *handy-man* one shows up today."

"Well, keep hoping," I say, glancing sideways and pulling a silver snowman out of the ornament box. "Because that's all you've got to go off of."

"It *is* a season for hope," Macie adds.

"It is a season for haste," I say, changing the subject and glancing at my watch. "Where are the caterers?"

"They got here ten minutes ago," Tad replies, adding songs to the playlist. "Can't you hear them poking around out front?"

I cannot. But I go to the door and sure enough, they're hauling boxes out of a van. "Perfect."

"A season for perfection," Becca hums.

"Panic," I reply, shuffling things around in order to make a path for the caterers.

"Magic," Macie chimes in as *The Nutcracker* pipes through the speakers.

"Indigestion," I counter.

"Splendor," Becca finishes as she steps back from the tree.

I don't have a retort because I pause too, admiring it. Macie comes over.

"Well, I think I learned you girls real good," I say, throwing out my best backwoods accent.

"Got that right," Macie replies. "If I'd done it without guidance it would have just looked like a kindergartener decorated it—the biggest, shiniest ornaments in big clusters everywhere."

"You know," I say. "That would have been pretty too." Then, looking around at the tables, I gasp. "Candles!"

"On it," Becca says, as I hurry into the kitchen to help the caterers.

t goes like that.

From candles to teacups to various bits of china from Memaw's collection. None of it matches, but that's okay because to it, I've added dozens of pieces from thrift shops in the area. Each time I bought a piece, I stayed for a spell, chatting with the owners and leaving fliers.

Exhausting, but kind of fun too.

I actually really liked getting to know them, digging through their things to find little treasures. Some of the shop owners were literally sitting on porch swings outside of their businesses, ready to talk. Others were a little more like me—business women and men with computerized logs and opinions about what belongs in a thrift shop—or emporium, as some of them called their businesses.

But something I noticed: I liked them all. From the guy who called both himself and his business (an old barn) Uncle Jesse to the fancy boutique-style second chance shops with the loftier names like The Frosted Crystal and Vintage Chic.

Second chance. I hadn't ever really thought I needed one. Swallowsville had been my second chance, and it had worked out great. But coming home, well, there's something about that too.

I push away thoughts of my, uh, third chance—of the job that will require me to move to Louisville, almost two hours away. In fact, I try not to think about my new job at all.

Instead, I wander around the furniture, keeping myself busy. Body moving, focused mind. Straightening tablecloths, adjusting bits of holly or pinecone that make up the centerpieces.

I've decorated in a way that could probably be called farmhouse chic. Brightly painted, antiqued wooden dressers, classic bed frames, long tables with benches and sturdy wooden chairs. Splashes of color. Vases with fresh flowers—red, silver, and glitter-themed, which I now accent with navy ribbons so they match the tree. Over all the windows are long gorgeous drapes, which I sewed myself with a few tips from Sally Mae. And, of course, the finished end tables I refurbished—again, giving me a chance to get to know the locals via their home stores and fix it shops.

The house is a whole series of second chances. Me, this stuff, the house itself.

I wasn't close enough to Memaw to imagine her smiling down on the whole thing. I mean, maybe she hates it. But, well, I can't help but appreciate the odd chance she gave me—to get to live a bit of country life with a bit of that side of the family—a side I thought had abandoned me forever.

It's not quite a neat circle of family—more like a series of messy, squiggly lines. But sometimes, like the piece of weird modern art that my family is, those lines still cross and come together.

CHAPTER 30

The biggest irony is that just as I'm enjoying this second chance with my hometown, I've lost my second chance with Jackson. If I ever really had one.

Too bad I was so resistant to taking that chance that he flew off to try a second chance with his sister's friend.

I sigh, stabbing another holly berry into a centerpiece.

And then the first guest arrives.

Shelby, from the gas station down the road—one of the places I frequented most often in all the days I've spent here, but not someone I thought would show up. "Miss Shelby," I say, taking her coat and giving it to one of the waiters, who's been assigned this job.

"Hey, baby. I just had to see what all the fuss was about. Looks like it was worth it."

She glances at her watch, and I feel it, the question on her mind that is also on mine. *Will anyone else arrive?* Won't be much of a gift to my hometown if they don't come enjoy it.

I swallow down the fear. "Coffee?" I ask her. "Or we've got tea or hot cocoa."

"You got a Dr. Pepper, baby?" she asks.

I swallow. "Afraid not," I say, letting my accent drip in. Am I still the wrong thing for this town?

"Well then, coffee will be just fine."

She settles into a sofa as the front door swings open again. Jesse from the thrift store, along with Maria from the shop down the road. They're having a heated discussion about lampshades or something. I smile, but don't interrupt.

Right behind them, I see several ladies I know are from the church—one the minister's wife. I smile as one of the ladies rushes to the tree. "Oh my heavens. Look at this one. It's just like my grandmamma used to have." She's pointing to one of the antique ornaments.

Sally Mae and her family arrive, wearing

matching fur hoods. Her two kids are cute, and also sort of matching—the girl in a dress, the boy wearing a bow tie with the same green and red pattern. Though I notice that he's also in little scuffed cowboy boots. So I guess even girl bosses lose some battles.

Sally Mae spots me and waves, her smile huge as she gestures to the house and gives me an enormous thumbs up.

The front door opens again and again and again. I lose track of the people, now crowding the room, drinking, laughing, standing shoulder to shoulder and cooing over the *hors d'oeuvres*.

But that doesn't mean I don't stop looking at the door. Not because I want to escape. The opposite really—because maybe I finally want to stay.

But how when I've accepted this new job, when everything is in place, when it pays more than I ever could have imagined making in my life?

When I turn again to the sound of the front door opening, I see Jackson standing there. Alone. No woman by his side. Maybe she's still not well enough to travel, or socialize. Somewhere in my head I remember that cancer patients have weakened immune systems.

I've only ever seen Jackson in jeans or scrubs, but

right now he's dressed to the hilt in a navy suit and tie. As though he planned to match the tree.

He's taking his mama's coat and nodding to the server. I just watch him for a moment—the smile, not wide, but deep, the copper eyes, that auburn swoop of hair, barely tamed enough to match his suit.

He turns to me, catches my eye (well, catches me staring if I'm honest). I walk over. "Looks like you're not planning on four wheeling," I say.

"I work at an ER," he replies. "So, nope. That kid's crazy."

He smiles. I smile.

And then there are guests guests guests. I'm greeting and chatting and pouring tea and refilling platters. Once I even caught a vase, like I belonged in a movie. The people around me actually clapped. I bowed. When I stood up, through all those laughing faces, I saw Jackson take his coat, kiss his mother's cheek, and walk toward the door.

The door. I excuse myself from the conversation I'm in with Harry from Home Depot and work my way as casually as I can toward the exit, but an older woman grabs my elbow and begins cooing about the lights. I catch one final glimpse of Jackson. He gives me a little smile, a quick wink, and then he's gone.

Into the cold December night.

I'm still nodding to the older lady, though I've lost track of what she's saying—something about how the bulbs used to be made of glass when she was a child.

I glance at Becca, who is talking to Lance, then to Macie, holding hands with Tad.

And I know I have to make my way to the door, for a little closure if nothing else.

The woman sees someone else she knows and makes a break from me.

I walk to the door, dancing my way through the crowd with noncommittal smiles and nods.

Through the open curtains, a light snow has begun to fall—magical fat flakes. I remember the way they piled up in heaps along the window panes in October. I remember moving the curtains, seeing the accumulation, hurrying to my car. And then the way we'd stood there for a moment—temporarily dazed, not by the snow, but by something else. Me gazing up, him gazing down. As though.... And then the shock of sound when Andy hit the house.

I step outside and don't see Jackson anywhere on the sidewalk or lawn, so I wrap an arm around one of the pillars on the porch, leaning my cheek against it. The bite of the cool wood feels good on my skin, at least for a moment.

Behind me, I hear a voice. "You're going to get cold."

I jump at the sound of his voice, and turn to see Jackson sitting on the porch swing. A few flakes have fallen into his hair, and I want to sweep them away.

Instead, I blush and say, "Oh, hey. I thought you'd left."

"Just getting a little fresh air."

"It is fresh," I reply. "Two snows already in southern Kentucky."

"Global warming," he replies.

"You know that sounds funny when we're watching it snow."

"I know," he says with a shrug. Then pats the spot beside him on the porch swing.

I pause, still clinging to the pillar. "Do you need to get home soon, to check on…" I realize I don't even know the woman's name. "…your friend's sister?"

"Haley?" he says. "Oh, she's not in town."

"I thought you were bringing her home to see your mama."

"She's still too weak to travel, and she wanted to

be with her family over the holidays anyway. She said we should aim for January."

"January sounds nice," I say, looking at the snow instead of into his face.

I can feel his eyes on me; I can hear the murmurs of people chatting inside. I'll have to get back soon.

Jackson pats the porch swing again, but I shake my head. "I better head back in. When Haley comes, I'd love to meet her. You can bring her here for a romantic dinner or something. My treat to thank you for all your help."

I turn to go inside and Jackson is staring at me with a funny look on his face. "Romantic?" he asks.

I glance back at him and shrug.

"Gretchen," he begins. "Come and sit down."

His voice is a little insistent. I glance in the door and see the guests, milling around, waiters taking care of them. No one is really missing me. That's as it should be. As it needs to be if I'm going to be working in Louisville.

"I—" I begin.

"Did you think that Haley and I...?" He leaves the question hanging, then pats the swing again.

Reluctantly, I sit. As far from him as I can.

"Did you think we were a couple?" he asks, turning to me.

"Well, of course," I say, glancing away, through one of the windows, which has a few snowflakes clinging to it, like I'd planned them in as part of the decorations. "You flew out to see her."

"She is an old family friend—my sister's best friend," he says. "That's all."

"What better person to fall in love with?" I ask.

He laughs then. "Gretchen, she's just twenty. Barely out of high school."

I shake my head, trying to put the words together, and he laughs harder. "And she's got a boyfriend—some guy who might try to put a ring on her finger this Christmas." He glances in the house, and smiles. "So maybe I *should* bring her here in a year or so. For their wedding. Your treat, you said?"

"I mean, I did say that," I reply, a little smile cracking on my face.

"Well, that is a deal. Told you small towns were filled with real nice people."

"Truly, you weren't wrong," I say, looking through the lighted window at a whole town who's shown up to support me. Me. The girl from the hills. Many of them know who my daddy was. Most of them knew grumpy ol' Memaw. They showed up anyway.

I wrap my sweater a little tighter around my body.

"And it's a real nice thing you've done for this town," he adds.

"Thank you," I say, and we both pause, silently watching the flakes fall, a little faster now.

"Does the snow give you PTSD?" I ask. "Not the real kind," I say, remembering he's a nurse. "But you know what I mean."

"Not too much," he says. "I've always loved the snow. There's something about it. It slows people down, quiets them, gives people permission to stay in, read a book…"

"…care for broken and bleeding joy riders."

"Of course. And look at all the cool stuff that came from that."

"I've got a brother now," I say, realizing I've shifted closer to the warmth that is Jackson, that there is very little space left between the two of us on the swing. He uses his foot to push the swing and we sway gently back and forth.

"Brother and business partner," he says.

I nod. "We're both good at it—business."

"You are," he agrees.

The snow is starting to accumulate on the cold

ground, flakes hanging off the Christmas lights, making their glow blur and soften.

Jackson reaches up, touching a snowflake, which melts quickly on his finger. "They're so beautiful," he says, "but one touch and they melt away."

"They're not to be held," I say.

"Fleeting," he murmurs.

"Which doesn't mean that the things that come from snow are fleeting," I add.

"What do you mean?" he asks, noticing the goosebumps on my neck. "Here, take my coat."

I hold a hand up to stop him, but he's already got it halfway onto my shoulders.

"Thank you," I say. "And I mean, look what came from that first snow. Andy, of course. He's the most obvious. And now we rent part of this property together, work together. I'm getting to know his mama too. And that's nice. I haven't had any kind of Mama in my life for seventeen years."

He nods and I wrap the coat tightly around my body.

"Go on," he says.

I shrug. "And the house, I guess. I mean, I already had it, and plans for it, but something about that day —being shut up with... Well, being stuck here together with Andy in such bad condition. It made me appreciate the beauty of it. When you and I had that argument about things being too country here —" I feel the heat of a blush rise up from my neck. "—I think that was me resisting this house, this city that I knew was so beautiful."

"You didn't resist for long," he says, gazing at the windows, smattered with flakes.

I clear my throat, thinking about my new job. "I knew it had potential," I say. "I always knew that. But that night I knew it had something else too."

"Home?" he asks.

"Maybe," I murmur, feeling my throat close off at the thought of living in Louisville, of being away from here except for the occasional weekend. "I guess I learned that I don't always know better. That's what I got from snow." I pause, barely daring to look at him. "What about you?"

He doesn't answer right away. I feel the swing tipping back and forth, back and forth. The snow makes everything around us even quieter than usual.

"Well, I saved a boy from dying," he said. "That was a good start."

I nod, turning to see the precise lines of his profile—a sharp nose, soft lips, wrinkles along his forehead like he wasn't done talking, wasn't done thinking.

"And a reminder that a cage in the middle of a forest is still a cage for the bird who can't fly away."

His eyes are dark against the glow of the porch lights.

"Jackson," I say, reaching up to touch his face, to turn it to mine, then stopping, tucking both my hands into the sleeves of his coat.

The swing tips back and forth, but I can feel it slowing, like a ride coming to an end.

"Sometimes birds, they break out of cages," I say.

"But then," he asks. "Do they fly away?"

"Yes," I say, thinking of Louisville, my paycheck, the grumpy faces of the people in the stores. Each part of the job so different than what I had expected. "But sometimes they also come back. It's what birds do."

"And people?" he asks, finally turning to me.

"Are more complicated than birds," I answer. "They stay when they shouldn't, hide when it's safer to run, and run when, well, they run a lot."

"They do," he says. The swing stops, hovers. He doesn't put a foot down to start it again.

"I'm glad we became friends," I say. "That's something else I got from the snow."

He reaches up to my hair, brushes a snowflake

onto his finger. We watch it—the intricacies fading and melting until it is nothing more than a droplet.

The door opens with a clang and a couple hurries out.

"You'd better get back," Jackson says. "They'll all be leaving soon. To beat the snow."

I stand, my face away from the lights, take off his coat and hand it back to him. "This porch is always here. If you need to swing," I say.

"Now that's an offer that's hard to refuse."

<hr>

In what feels like minutes, though it's probably closer to an hour, the guests have cleared, leaving me with empty tea cups and crumpled napkins. I peek out the window. One last time.

Jackson is gone.

Macie and Tad are bundling up.

"You sure you want to go?" I ask. "You could stay for the night."

"We've got work tomorrow," Macie says. "And the kitties will miss us. Besides, who knows how much worse this will get. I don't want to get stranded."

"Ah, it's not so bad," I say. "Especially now that I have the cupboards stocked with more than just Cheez-its."

"What's that?" Becca asks, tugging at something around my neck. I look down to see Jackson's black scarf. He must have put it on with the coat.

I reach up and touch it. In the bustle, I hadn't even noticed it was there.

Lance hands Becca her coat. "We should get off too," he says.

But Becca is still staring at me. "You didn't answer," she says.

"It's a scarf," I answer.

"That you weren't wearing before," she says.

"Jackson lent it to me when I went outside for some fresh air."

Macie and Becca both swivel to me like they're the spotlights of an interrogation.

"Well, you better return it," Becca says, glancing at the porch. "The night is still young."

"I don't even know where he lives," I say.

"Oh, I do," Macie says. "I was chatting with his mom."

"Small towns," I grumble. "Who just gives out someone's address?"

"Mothers do," Becca answers. "I'm surprised

Lance's mom didn't put his on Facebook with a personals ad back when he was single."

"She did once start a Tinder account for me," Lance says. "Put me up there in my uniform, along with loads of baby pictures. Which could have gotten me fired, by the way—with the uniform up there and all. So we shut it down real quick."

"I'm texting you the address," Macie says, her face in her phone.

"I can't just show up there," I say. "It's creepy."

"You can't steal a scarf," Macie replies. "That's theft, and Tad and I work for law enforcement."

"Besides," Becca says. "You're spending the night here, so no rush to leave."

I look around. "I've got to clean this up."

"You need anything before I go?" Andy says, popping his head in the back door.

"Gretchen needs you to help clean up so she can return this stolen scarf to Jackson," Macie says, not missing a beat.

"On it," Andy answers, taking off his coat.

"It's not stolen," I say, my voice rising. "And I'll help you clean."

"It's just some paper, trash, and dishes. Mama made me do dishes every night of my life. I suppose I can do a few more," Andy says.

"There's soap under the sink," Becca replies. "And we'll help so it goes faster."

"Thought you had to beat the snow," I say.

"It's just an inch," Lance pipes up.

"Two," I counter.

Tad is rolling up his sleeves, feeling around for paper products. "I've got trash if you guys do dishes."

"Go," Macie says to me.

The tears prick into my eyes before I can stop them.

"None of that," Becca says, shoving me toward the door.

The snow isn't really accumulating much, but it's still beautiful, falling in whirls around my face. According to my GPS, Jackson's house is just a couple miles away. All this time, and I didn't know he was practically my neighbor. "I'm walking," I text my friends, so they won't panic if they see my car.

"You're stalling," Becca replies.

But I'm not, not really. I'm letting the silence in, allowing the snow to still my thoughts, my mood. Just like Jackson said it did.

Each step I take leaves a small, quiet imprint in my path. I had thought I would use the time to compose a little speech, find a non-awkward way to return the scarf. Instead, I use it to let my thoughts fly away—they themselves like snowflakes. Here, then gone. Beautiful, impermanent things.

And then I notice the other set of prints in the snow, faded a bit as more flakes had fallen, though more defined the closer I get to Jackson's house. His own footprints. Still fresh. Until they stop.

"Good thing I gave you that scarf," I hear him say from a place on his porch. "Otherwise, you'd catch your death." He says it in a perfect imitation of motherly drawl.

I can barely see him in the darkness of his house. "Macie said I had to return the stolen goods," I say, unwinding the scarf.

"You should keep it," he says. "Looks better on you than me."

"I doubt that," I say, standing at the bottom of three steps.

He stands and I see him in the light sky of a snowy night—still in his suit, but wrapped up in a quilt. "Come on up."

"Why aren't you inside?" I ask, sitting on the stoop of the porch beside him.

"I wanted to think," he answers. "And what better night for it?"

"Same reason I walked here then," I reply.

"Is it the same reason?" he asks.

"Thinking," I answer.

"About?" he asks.

"The country, the snow," I say.

"I was thinking about birds," he replies. "They like to spread their wings. And it's a beautiful thing —a bird on the wing."

"It is," I answer. "No birds out tonight though. Not even an owl."

"There's one," he answers, looking straight into my face. "It's scary when you know a bird can fly off. Especially when you're more of a sluggish land mammal yourself."

"This metaphor is getting weird," I say, smiling.

From the top of the blanket, I can see he's in his white shirt still, though the tie's gone, the top button undone. "Truth is, I'm having trouble saying anything directly."

"Then let's just watch the snow," I reply.

He nods. I wrap myself into my coat, looking more like a turtle than a bird.

He smiles at me, a sideways thing. "You know, there's room in here," he says, opening the blanket.

"Plenty of room," he says quickly. "No excessive closeness required."

"That is maybe the worst line I've ever heard," I say, scooting closer, letting him drape the blanket over my shoulders.

"Pick-up lines are not my forte. Women are not my forte."

I settle closer to him. "What is your forte?" I ask.

"I don't know," he says. "Working hard. Running. Not away, exactly. Not like some." He gives me that sideways grin again. "But running. Hamster style, on a wheel. Keeping busy."

"Accomplishing things," I add.

"True," he says. "Good things. But running's running."

I nestle next to his side, feeling the warmth, and he wraps the blanket tighter around my shoulders, sealing us in against the cold.

The snow drifts lazily, not at all down to business like it was on that first night when we got trapped. Not filling up, just swirling around, settling on things, then flitting away in the breeze.

"A night like this," I say. "It's a night like forever. A night you could stay in."

"Could you?" he asks.

I turn my face to his, our lips a breath apart.

Could I?

His lips are warm, even in the cold, working over my mouth, my cheeks, my jaw—our bodies tight in the cocoon of the blanket. Flushing, hot.

He pulls away, rubbing both thumbs against my cheeks. I reach up a hand to his hand, lean against it.

He kisses my forehead, my chin, my throat.

"We're going to melt all the snow," I say, smiling.

"We should have tried that when we were stuck in your house," he says, kissing me again, each touch like a flame dancing along my skin.

I press against him, the blanket slipping from my shoulders.

And then a horn blares down the street. We both jump, then laugh.

"I better get you home," Jackson says, standing and holding out his hand. "It's a small town."

"Small towns," I grumble. "I told you they were trouble."

"Yeah, we're pretty much going to make the front page of the newspaper at this rate." He opens the front door and grabs a coat.

"Well," I say. "At least that will be some publicity for Gretchen's Cottage. *Loose Woman Seduces Town Nurse.*"

"*Make Out in Handmade Quilt,*" Jackson continues.

"*In the Middle of Blazing Snowstorm,*" I finish.

"Ah, this time it isn't the storm that's blazing," Jackson says in that sugar drawl. He wraps his scarf back around my neck, pulling me in for a last slow kiss, then takes my hand as we walk down the street. "Told you good things come from snow."

What can I say?

He was right.

EPILOGUE

I drive for the last time from Louisville to Midvale.

And who does that? Who gives up a profitable job to be closer to her little startup business?

"You doing okay, Boss Girl?" Becca texts me as I pull into the empty parking lot.

"You mean Lover Girl," Macie chimes in to the group text.

"You can be both!" Becca texts back.

I turn off my car as a male cardinal swoops in front of me, landing on a little patch of snow that still dots the periphery. Newscasters were calling it the worst winter Kentucky has seen in nearly half a century. When the groundhog came out last week and didn't see his shadow, Midvale even had a parade. A parade I missed because I was at work in a skyscraper in Louisville.

And maybe the groundhog was right because, even though the sky is gray and it's supposed to snow again tonight, that little cardinal is tugging at a bit of seed from among the snowy grass.

"I'm turning you guys off for a while," I text. "And, yeah, I'm doing okay. Better than okay."

I click my phone off, take a deep breath, and get out of my car.

Jackson is standing near the cast iron gate, waiting with two carnations in his hands. Flowers that are not for me.

"You ready?" he asks.

"Getting it all over with all in one day," I say.

"It'll take more than a day," he replies with a crooked little smile. "To get it all processed."

"Well, then, let's get started."

"That's my little Type A princess," he says.

We wander through the cemetery for a solid twenty minutes before I find them—two tombstones, side by side. Eddie Pearson Stephens. Roberta Stephens.

I cock my head to the side, looking at the stones. Jackson is clearing the graves with some clippers he brought, making everything look as nice as possible.

But I'm just staring. These aren't the little flat head-stones that most people have. They're upright, and my daddy's has a delicate cross engraved into the top.

I realize, as I wouldn't have when I was younger, that my parents couldn't have had the money—much less the foresight—to buy cemetery plots. And Mama's mama was long dead. And no granddaddies were ever in the picture—at least as long as I can remember.

Which leaves only one person.

Memaw must have bought this little plot.

Which means that she might be nearby.

Her stone is small, unassuming. It *is* one of the flat ones you could almost step over and not notice.

Jackson comes up behind me as I stare. "Well, I'll be," he says. His hands are pink from the dropping temperatures, and he digs around in his coat for a pair of gloves.

I stop him, taking his hand in mine, warming it that way.

You can tell that Memaw's grave isn't nearly as overgrown as Mama and Daddy's. Not nearly as old.

We stand staring for several minutes. And then I wander around, looking for my granddaddy, wondering if I'll ever have an answer to that mystery in Memaw's life.

But Memaw is alone. "He must have left," I say. "When they were young."

"Or he's hidden here," Jackson says. "Under some name we don't know."

I nod, but there's something in me that knows he isn't. Something in that bent diamond ring. In the fatherless portraits I saved from Memaw's house.

Back when I'd taken the ring to the jeweler, she'd told me not to sell it until I at least learned its story. Which means I won't be selling it anytime soon. But that's okay. Because maybe that ring needs a new story, not an old one.

Jackson puts his arm around me, and I let the weight, the surety of that arm, ground me. "You wanting to run away again?" he asks softly.

"A little," I say, as the wind starts to pick up. "Coming home means facing a lot of hurts. It'd be easier to run."

"Ah, Gretchen," he says. "Not when you've got wings to fly."

"I could use them to fly away again," I say.

"You could," he answers. "But I think you're going to use them to fly high. To do big things."

"I just gave up a big thing," I say, staring at the graves.

"To make something even bigger. I've been talking to Andy. He says you've got plans."

"You can't make a big thing from a small place," I say, remembering the first time I realized it.

"And you can't do big things without being a big person," he answers. "Not literally, of course."

He wraps his arms against my waist, pulling me in. I nestle against his neck, against his warmth. As I do, an icy breeze blows through the trees, pushing us even closer to the safety that is each other.

The wind carries a few little crystals, which settle against Jackson's cheek. Perfect flakes. Melting into delicate drops.

And I remember everything I've gained. From snow.

ACKNOWLEDGMENTS

Huge thank you to all the friends and family who have supported me in the writing of my books—my husband and kids, as well as my siblings and friends.

Thank you to my editor, Carrie.

And to my cover designer, Les.

An extra thank you to my fix-it husband, Kip (who is also a paramedic) from whom I have learned how to fix houses (okay, I'm more of a helper) as well as how to fix bodies that are broken or bleeding. And please know that any errors I've got in this book about fixing stuff or helping with broken femurs are due to my own misunderstanding.

J. E. Pace is the author of the books *From Ashes, From Gunpowder, From Asphalt,* and the short story "Ready," which you can get for free by signing up for her newsletter.

If you enjoy fantasy or memoir, you can find more of her work, written under the name Jean Knight Pace.